SHEENA WILKINSON

Little
Island

STAR BY STAR

First published in 2017 by
Little Island Books
7 Kenilworth Park
Dublin 6W
Ireland

ISBN: 978-1-910411-53-7

A British Library Cataloguing in Publication record for this book is available from the British Library.

Cover illustration by Niall McCormack
Insides designed and typeset by www.redrattledesign.com

Printed in Poland by Drukarnia Skleniarz

Little Island receives financial assistance from
The Arts Council/An Chomhairle Ealaíon and the Arts Council of Northern Ireland

10 9 8 7 6 5 4 3 2 1

For Julie McDonald, who loves books and history

Historical Note

Star by Star is set in winter 1918, when a great deal was happening in Ireland and beyond: the end of the Great War; the flu pandemic; Irish independence; and women's suffrage – the right to vote.

The Great War – which we now call the First World War – was limping to its end in autumn 1918. In over four years, it had killed and maimed millions of young men. By the time the Armistice was signed on 11 November 1918 the world was exhausted.

And not only by war. The influenza pandemic of 1918–19 was one of the most devastating episodes in human history. It killed upwards of 50 million people worldwide, many more than died in the war. Unlike most strains of influenza, which prey on the old and weak, this flu virus killed a lot of young people. It could strike terrifyingly quickly, and there are many stories of people dropping dead in the street. Sometimes it is called Spanish Flu, because it was first reported in a Spanish newspaper. Ireland was as badly affected as anywhere else, with more than 20,000 deaths.

Before the war, Ireland, which was at the time ruled by Britain, had been on the brink of Home Rule, which meant that Ireland would be given a large degree of independence, though it would still be answerable to the British parliament. This was postponed because of the war, which, of course, nobody in 1914 expected to last so long.

At the time of the 1916 Easter Rising, a rebellion against British rule in Ireland, many people on both sides of the Irish Sea regarded rebelling during the war, when thousands of Irishmen from all backgrounds were fighting with the British army, as betrayal. However, by 1918 the tide of nationalist opinion was turning. Britain's attempts in 1918 to introduce conscription to force Irishmen to fight helped increase support for Sinn Féin, who wanted complete independence from Britain rather than merely Home Rule.

At the General Election in December 1918, Sinn Féin had a landslide victory in Ireland, including in parts of Ulster. The first woman to be elected was a Sinn Féin candidate, Constance Markiewicz, but as an Irish republican she did not take her seat in Westminster: Sinn Féin instead established their own parliament, Dáil Éireann, in Dublin. It would be several years, though, and much more bloodshed before Ireland – or at least 26 counties – gained independence from Britain and formed the Irish Free State.

In the past, only men who owned property could vote in elections. Women had fought for the vote since the 1870s, but the campaign for women's suffrage really took off in the early twentieth century. Finally in 1918 the right to vote was extended to all men over 21, and to women over 30 who were householders or married to householders.

There were many women's suffrage societies, in both Britain and Ireland, with differing ideas about how to fight for the vote. The best-known was the Women's Social and Political Union, led by Mrs Emmeline Pankhurst and Christabel, one of her daughters. The WSPU, frustrated with peaceful tactics being ignored, embarked on direct action, with their slogan 'Deeds Not Words'. They targeted public buildings, smashed windows and set fire to postboxes, and many were imprisoned for their actions. When the Great War broke out in August 1914, the WSPU suspended their campaign and threw their energies into supporting the war. But many suffragists opposed the war, which led to disagreements within the movement.

In the Irish Free State women achieved equal voting rights in 1922, whereas in Britain they had to wait until 1928. The very first country to enfranchise women was New Zealand, in 1893, while women in Saudi Arabia were not granted the vote until 2015.

It's thirty years since I first voted, in the 1987 UK General Election, and as I walked to the polling station that day I remembered the women who fought, suffered and even died so that I could exercise that right. I still think of them, every time I cast my vote.

Sheena Wilkinson

Co Down

June 2017

1

The carriage was nearly empty. By the time the train was shuddering along the coast towards Cuanbeg, rain lashing the windows, there was only me and the girl in the navy coat left. She looked like a girl in a school story, with her neat brown plait. I'd grown out of school stories but I couldn't help wishing I had one now, instead of only a *Belfast Telegraph* someone had left behind. The print was so tiny that my eyes and brain hurt. I laid it down with an exaggerated sigh, and, as I'd hoped, she looked up from her own paper.

'War and flu,' I said. 'As usual. Though they say the war's going to end soon.'

She gave a tight smile and half-turned to look out the window, even though there was nothing to see but streaming rain and a moody pewter sea.

I tried again. 'And a man's died aged 108. If *I* lived to that age, I'd die in … um – 2011. Doesn't that sound crazy?'

'Yes.' But she didn't say it in an inviting way and picked up her own paper again. The *Irish Citizen*.

I gave a squeak of recognition. 'We have that!' I said. 'At least – we used to.' Mam's friend Rose sometimes had it sent over from Belfast. But after their big fight she'd disappeared, and I hadn't seen it since. Now it looked like an old friend.

'Are you a suffragist, then?'

'Of course!' I pulled back my woollen scarf and showed her the little green, purple and white WSPU badge on the lapel of my coat. The girl gave a smile that brightened her face. She turned up her coat collar. She had exactly the same badge! Only hers was pinned back-to-front so it couldn't be seen.

'I came straight from school,' she said. 'I've got into trouble so often that I have to wear it in secret.' She unpinned and refastened it to the front of her collar.

'I'd hate that,' I said. 'I never hide my beliefs.' Then, in case she'd think I was criticising, I added: 'Of course I've left school, which makes it easier.' I tossed my bobbed hair and hoped she would think how grown-up I looked.

'Mama hates it too.' She sighed. 'Doesn't yours?'

'Some of my earliest memories are of Mam taking me to suffragette rallies. When other girls were embroidering samplers, I was stitching VOTES FOR WOMEN onto banners.' My voice caught and I looked down at my lap.

'Lucky you! I wish my mother was like that.'

I swallowed hard. If she asked any more I would have to say Mam was dead. And then I might cry, and I never cried. Not even this morning, sitting on my suitcase on the quayside, still queasy from the rough crossing from

Liverpool, getting colder and colder and crosser and crosser, and maybe a *tiny* bit scared at being all on my own in this strange country. The crowds had thinned, and people were staring and in the end I had stood up, tilted my chin so nobody could feel sorry for me, and strolled off in the direction of the train station as if this had been my intention all along and I'd merely been sitting on my suitcase for half an hour to admire the beauty of the Belfast Quay on a damp October morning.

Surely Nancy would be at Cuanbeg station! I had sent a wire: *You didn't meet boat so taking train. Arrives 1.05 p.m. Stella Graham.* I had added *Graham* despite its costing extra, even though she would know perfectly well who I was, because I didn't want to be too friendly to someone who'd left her own niece sitting for hours on the quayside in the rain. It wasn't very aunt-like behaviour and she should know I wasn't impressed. Not that I thought of her as *Aunt* Nancy: I'd never met her, and I wasn't used to family. Except Mam.

I longed to keep talking to the girl but I couldn't trust myself to speak, so I pretended to read the *Belfast Telegraph* again, and she took the hint and went back to the *Irish Citizen*. She must have thought me peculiar, but at least I hadn't blubbed.

The train listed round a corner and juddered to a stop with a screech of brakes. Cuanbeg! The girl leapt to the door as if she couldn't wait to get off. 'Bye!' she said, and was swallowed by the smoke and steam. Probably she was being whisked away by loving parents, perhaps even in a motorcar, and was on her way to toasted teacakes by the fireside. (It was more like lunchtime, but travelling all night had made me lose all sense of time.) *She* wasn't going to an unknown cruel aunt who only wanted her to skivvy in her rotten seaside boarding house. Probably I wouldn't meet her again, even in a small town. If her mam didn't like suffragists, she wouldn't approve of me.

My suitcase seemed to have got heavier on the journey, and I had to buckle the strap tighter round it because it had been threatening to burst all the way from Manchester. I didn't trust it not to let me down at this final stage. By the time I'd dragged it from the luggage rack and off the train the steam and smoke had cleared and the platform was empty of aunts or any other human life. The wind whipped up my coat and I jammed my woollen beret down firmer. Even though there was nobody in sight I tried to look as if I wasn't worried, but inside fear bubbled. *What if Aunt Nancy never turns up? And I'm stranded in this place for ever, all alone? What can have happened to prevent her meeting me?*

The most likely explanation was –

The bubble of fear swelled into a balloon. No! Not again. And yet, *why* not? It was happening all over the country – schools closed, unburied bodies piled high, people dropping dead in the streets …

I decided the balloonish feeling was hunger. Things wouldn't be solved by a bun and a cup of tea but they would be improved. The station buffet was tiny, and I had to ask three times before the woman understood my accent, but there was a tiny fire, and soon I was sitting at a scuffed wooden table with my suitcase at my feet and a thick white china mug warming my hands.

If Aunt Nancy *had* died, it would be terrible. And extremely inconvenient when she was my only living relative. But I'd never met her, so it couldn't be a *personal* sorrow. And perhaps she would have left me something in her will, and I could use it to make my way in life. I wasn't sure what my way in life would be, but it had to be better than slaving away in a seaside boarding house. Cliffside House was probably just a draughtier version of 17 Eupatoria Street, where Mam and I had lived in Manchester.

I felt forsaken, but noble and determined, a cross between Anne of Green Gables and Joan of Arc.

I didn't rush my bun. I still hoped that at any minute the door might fly open and a kind, smiling aunt rush in, full of apologies and welcome, and I wouldn't have to make my way all alone *just* yet. But the door stayed shut, and the waitress wiped the counter and sniffed, and my tea was finished and I hadn't enough money for another.

So there was nothing to do but lift up my suitcase and my chin and ask the waitress, 'Do you know Cliffside House?'

'Aye,' she said, wiping and sniffing.

Hope flickered. She didn't say, *Are you here for the funeral? Wasn't it a tragedy?* Then again, Aunt Nancy might have died that very morning. 'Could you tell me how to get there?'

She frowned at my suitcase. 'It's a fair way.'

'I've come all the way from Manchester on my own.' I couldn't keep the pride out of my voice, but she didn't look as impressed as she should have done, though she looked at me carefully as if trying to place me.

'Follow the coast to the end of the harbour, and then take Cliff Road – on your right. Keep going uphill. You'll see a ruined cottage at a crossroads. Take the wee loaning on the left. That'll take you straight to the house.'

I'd no idea what a *wee loaning* was, but if I got that far I could always ask somebody else.

'Thanks.'

And armed with my suitcase, a salty-sharp sea breeze pulling at my beret, I set off.

2

Cuanbeg was just a sweep round the bay, with a stone harbour at one end, and a few streets of terraced houses leading off. The cliffs glowered over the town like huge grey mills. The shops and cafés on the front mostly had their shutters down – for lunch, or half-day closing, or because it was winter, I didn't know.

The water slapped against the sea wall, scraps of weed floating in its scum like bits of leek in soup. Mam must have walked along this coast road when she was my age, and looked across the water, fantasising about escape. 'Me and Rose,' she'd say. 'Two wild dreamers!' Used to terraced streets safely walled in by mills and factories and shops, I felt exposed and small.

At first the cliff road rose gently, with big pastel-coloured villas whose green lawns swept down to the sea. One, painted pink like an iced birthday cake, had a long veranda, with wheelchairs lined up, and in every wheelchair was a young man with a blanket over his lap and, as far as I could see – though I tried not to stare – not much evidence of anything under the blanket. The house was called 'Sunny View', but the view wasn't sunny today. The blast coming off the sea made my ears scream even with my hat pulled down. Poor wounded soldiers: maimed in a hideous war and then parked in front of a sullen grey sea. I hawked my suitcase more determinedly; I bet there wasn't one man on that veranda who wouldn't have switched places with me.

The houses ended, and the road got rougher underfoot, and so steep I kept having to stop, set my case down and rub my aching shoulder. Every time I picked up my case again the handle creaked. Up here the wind wasn't so fierce, and tangled, straggling hedges blocked out the sea. I'd imagined somewhere more like Blackpool. *I'm trying to make a go of Cliffside as a boarding house,* Nancy had written, *as it's far too big for me on my own and I don't want to sell it. It's a little way out of town so it attracts people wanting a quieter stay.* A little way!

Just when I thought my lungs would burst and my arms drop off, I saw, peeping from behind an overgrown fuchsia, a tumbled pile of grey stone, still recognisable as a cottage. Jags of broken glass clung to rotten window-frames, and blackened rags of thatch fringed the rafters. This was where I had to look out for a *wee loaning*. I was starting to feel that the whole world was playing a joke on me, and that I was being magicked into some weird Irish fairyland, but sure enough, past the crossroads a few steps on from the cottage, was a definite path. And attached to a gnarled tree was a painted wooden sign: *Cliffside House*. Whatever awaited me there, at least my journey was nearly over.

But not quite. Turning into the lane, I saw the house ahead. I had barely time to notice that it was grey and square, before I heard a terrible sobbing. Then, hurtling towards me, plait bouncing round her shoulders, face mottled with tears, came the girl from the train.

3

The path was so narrow she'd crash into me. I leapt into the bushes, and my suitcase handle gave up the ghost. It snapped, and the case bashed to the ground, spilling clothes over the stony lane, and stopping the girl in her tracks. I dropped to my knees and started gathering everything up, and she caught her breath with a gulp and knelt down to help.

'Are you all right?' I asked as she handed me my good grey frock and my favourite old red jumper.

She blinked the tears away. 'Fine.'

The balloon of fear started swelling again, because whatever was making her cry was obviously something to do with Cliffside House. She took a long, ragged breath that reminded me of Mam struggling to breathe that last day. *No, no, push that away.*

'I'm sorry,' she said. 'I shouldn't get so upset. I don't normally.'

'Has someone died?'

'No,' she said. She pulled back her cuff to check her

wristwatch. 'I should go. If I miss the three o'clock there isn't another train until six.'

'You don't live in Cuanbeg?' I tried to keep the disappointment from my voice.

She shook her head. 'My cousin does.' She jerked her head back towards Cliffside House.

For a moment I thought she meant Aunt Nancy, and that might mean *we* were somehow related. Hope sparked. But then she said, 'He won't even *see* me.' Fresh tears welled in her eyes, making them huge and dark in her pale face. She glanced at her watch again and said, 'Look, I *must* go. Sorry again.'

'Are you coming back some time?' I asked. 'I'm going to live here. At Cliffside House, I mean.'

'Aren't you a bit young to be living in rooms? Or are you going to work here?'

I tilted my chin. Had she noticed how shabby my coat was? 'Actually, no to both,' I said. 'I've travelled on my own from Manchester. I'm all alone in the world.' I hoped this sounded romantic. 'Miss Graham's my aunt. I'm Stella Graham.'

'I see.' She bit her lip. 'No, I don't think I'll come back. Maybe it's time to give up.'

'Never give up until you're dead,' I said. That's what Mam always told me.

She smiled, a wintry smile. 'I don't usually.'

'Me neither.' This time we both smiled, and I wished she wasn't rushing off. I missed talking to people my own age. I hadn't even been able to say goodbye to Sadie and Lil, my friends at the commercial college. 'Look – before you go,' I said. 'Is Nancy – Miss Graham – all right? She didn't meet me.'

'Oh, she's out. Friday's her day helping at Sunny View. That's where she first met my cousin,' she explained.

'Ah.' Out doing Good Works! All very well, but it would have been a better work to have gone to Belfast to meet her poor orphaned niece. Still, at least she wasn't dead.

'I must go,' the girl said. 'And – no' – she squared her shoulders as if making a decision – 'I won't come back. Unless he asks me to. There's not giving up and then – well, there's making an idiot out of yourself. Flogging a dead horse.'

Even though I had just met her, I felt a wrench.

'What's your name?' I asked.

'Helen Reid,' she said. 'My cousin's Sandy Reid.' She scrabbled in her pocket and took out a packet of cigarettes. 'Could you give him these? I didn't get a chance.'

I took the cigarettes. I didn't like the sound of Sandy, but I liked having a task for Helen. Then she really did dash off to get her train and I clutched my battle-scarred suitcase for the last lap of my journey to the square grey house that didn't, the nearer I got, look any more welcoming.

4

Where the path met Cliffside House's gate, I could see the sea again, and feel its salty bite on my cheeks. Beyond a small lawn, the land sloped sharply downhill. I looked up at the house. Grey and solid, it wasn't smart like Sunny View, but neither was it sooty and flaking like the thin terraced houses of Eupatoria Street. Two bay windows on the ground floor, three plain ones on the floor above, and two little attic ones stared hard at the sea. I thought I saw someone standing at one of the attic windows, but it might have been a shadow.

I set my case down on the doorstep, and leaned forward to press the doorbell on the white-painted front door. It rang through the rooms, then died into silence. Nobody came. Great. So there wasn't even a maid. Not that I was used to maids. But in a house this size! No wonder Aunt Nancy had been *longing to meet me*. Longing to make use of me, more likely. I wanted to stamp my foot and swear and catch the next train out of this windy grey place and back to my old life.

So why didn't I? I wasn't a child. I was fifteen. I'd left school and had been learning shorthand and typing so I could get a job in an office instead of having to go into a factory. So why had I crossed the sea and spent hours in a draughty train and trudged up a steep blooming *loaning* to this gloomy house and an aunt I'd never met and who couldn't want me as much as she'd claimed? Why not stay in Manchester?

It was a deathbed promise. Much less romantic than it sounds. Mam didn't drop dead in the street like some people with this terrible flu. She was ill for a couple of days, sweating and coughing and screaming with pain. The night before she died, fingers plucking the counterpane, a purple shadow spreading from her lips across her cheeks, I think she *knew*. She said, struggling between coughs for every word: 'Don't stay here alone, Stella, love. Go home to Ireland. To your aunt.'

Ireland wasn't *home*; it was only the place that had spat my mother out when she was a terrified girl in trouble. And Aunt Nancy was no more than a name on a birthday card and the occasional letter. The only Irish person I really knew was Rose Sullivan, but we hadn't heard from Rose since they'd had their big fight back in 1914. I thought she'd gone back to Belfast.

But even I wasn't going to argue in the circumstances, so I'd said, 'You're going to get better.'

Mam shook her head. 'Promise,' she whispered. And then she had been racked by the worst coughing yet, until her body arched like a vomiting cat's, and blood spurted from her mouth and nose all over the rose-patterned counterpane. And that was the last time she spoke.

You can't break a deathbed promise, I thought, as I pulled off my hat and raked my fingers through my sweaty hair. Anyway, Mrs Myatt, the landlady in Eupatoria Street, had said she wasn't having a skit of a lass all alone in the rooms and she wanted them for munitions workers. Which was a lie – everyone said the war would end soon; I think she just thought I'd be trouble. But once the funeral was paid for, there hadn't been any money. Only a letter from Aunt Nancy, with my fare, saying I must come to Cuanbeg at once.

I've always longed to meet you, she had written. Not enough to come to the station, let alone the quayside!

And then I heard, from inside the house, an uneven shuffling thud and the creaking of wood. Someone was coming slowly – and painfully, it sounded – down the stairs, clutching the rail for support. Sandy! Hadn't Nancy met him in Sunny View? I thought of all those soldiers plonked on the veranda, hardly a limb between them. Sandy must have only one leg. I imagined him hobbling downstairs, cursing another interruption. He had refused even to *see* Helen, and she was his cousin. As the faltering steps came closer, I swallowed, preparing for a cross between Heathcliff and Long John Silver. But I was indignant enough by now to give as good as I got.

'Stella? Och, you poor wee thing.'

I blinked.

A little old lady stood in the doorway. She was leaning

on a stick, dressed in a long black gown and a mauve woollen shawl. Her wrinkled face creased at the sight of me. 'We didn't expect you till tomorrow! You haven't come all this way on your own? Dear bless us! Aren't the young girls these days powerful?' She shook her head in wonder.

Immediately I felt proud. And so relieved I'd have burst into tears if I'd been that kind of girl. I'd never had a granny – well, not one who'd acknowledge my existence – but all at once I wanted this old dear to be my gran. She was like a granny in a story, with a silvery plait wrapped round her head.

She pulled the door wider. 'Come on in,' she said. 'Nancy was all set to go up to Belfast in the morning. She was going to take the motorcar on its first proper expedition. Safer than breathing in all those germs on the train. But here you are, all on your own!'

A *motorcar*? I hadn't dreamed of such a thing. I'd yearned, for years, for a bicycle, but we'd never been able to manage one, though I could ride one, after a fashion, because Lil sometimes borrowed her sister's and let me have a go. 'I said I was arriving today,' I said. 'The 26th.'

'Och, dear, it's only the 25th.'

'Really?' I rubbed my eyes. Maybe it was. Everything had happened so fast – Mam's illness, when day and night had been one nightmare blur, and trying to arrange the funeral when all the undertakers in the city were up to their eyes, and Aunt Nancy's letter, and getting rid of Mam's bits and pieces, and packing, and finding out about boats …

I found myself blurting all of this out to the old lady,

standing in the oak-panelled hallway, and suddenly I didn't feel powerful, or cross, only wobbly legged and exhausted. 'I don't usually make stupid mistakes,' I said. 'I'm very sensible.'

'Of course you are. Didn't you get yourself all the way here?'

She helped me off with my coat, though she had to stretch up as I was a good bit taller, and drew me towards a door. 'Come and sit yourself down,' she said. 'Minnie can take your case up later. I don't know why she didn't hear the doorbell. Head in the clouds, no doubt.'

I didn't really listen, except to register that Minnie must be the maid. I was too busy looking round the sitting room. It was a hundred times more comfortable than anywhere I'd lived with Mam. We'd moved around a bit and the places were usually cramped and always damp. This room was large and square, with green velvet curtains hanging in the bay window. The furniture was old-fashioned, solid and cosy-looking. The fire was set, and the old lady took matches from a box on the mantelpiece and lit it, and it whooshed into life. Sitting neatly on the centre of the mantelpiece, in front of a china figurine, was a small beige envelope. My telegram!

She lowered herself into the larger of the armchairs, and gestured for me to sit in the other one, right beside the fire. She picked up some knitting from a basket beside the chair. People were always knitting dull khaki for soldiers, but the garment – too soon to tell what it was – that hung from her needles was soft and pink. 'I don't like being idle,' she said, when she saw me looking. 'I'll keep you company till your aunt comes home – unless you'd rather be on your own?'

'Oh, no,' I said.

'I'm one of your aunt's boarders,' she said, when she reached the end of a row. 'Miss Harriet McKay.' She smiled. 'I gave up my house last year, and this suits me well. I can see the sea even if my days of walking on the beach are over.' She gave a funny little twitch with her tartan-slippered feet.

'How many people live here?' I asked.

Miss McKay considered. 'Well, there's me, and young Mrs Phillips from Belfast; she's a widow, God love her. She's bad with her chest. She's here for the good air. This desperate flu.' She shook her head the way everyone did when they mentioned it. 'It's everywhere. Canada and Australia. I heard even the Eskimos have it.'

I chewed my lip.

She leant forward to look at me closely. 'You're pale, child. I hope *you're* not sickly?'

I shook my head. 'I'm naturally pale,' I said. 'But I'm very healthy. *And* I've had the flu already. But not badly.' Not like Mam.

'You'll get roses in your cheeks here,' Miss McKay said. 'Everyone does.' She rubbed her own papery cheek, and sure enough it was faintly pink under the wrinkles. 'Oh,' she said, her voice changing, 'and there's a young man up in the attic. He keeps to himself. Now' – she set her knitting down – 'I'll ring for tea. You must be ready for it. Imagine walking all this way!'

There was a bell hanging by the mantelpiece on a silk rope, and Miss McKay reached over and pulled it. Ringing for tea! Going to Belfast in a motorcar! When the door opened and a girl came in, in a print dress and a white apron, I felt like I'd landed in a different world. Mam had said her family was *respectable* and that's why they'd reacted so badly when she got into trouble. Girls like her weren't meant to have babies. But I hadn't guessed they were *posh*.

'I wonder you didn't hear the doorbell, Minnie,' Miss McKay said. 'Poor Stella here was stranded on the doorstep.'

'I was smoothing the Captain's sheets,' Minnie said. She ran her hands over her apron, and gave me a cool up-and-down glance. I remembered Helen thinking *I* was a maid and looked down at my tweed skirt. It had been new last year but it had gone baggy at the knees and was plucked in places. It was nowhere near as pretty as Minnie's dress, even though, closer up, I saw that sweat rings bloomed under her arms.

'On a Friday? And surely the sheets go out to the laundry?'

Minnie shrugged. She was plump and dark-eyed with bright red cheeks which might have been from the hot iron. 'There was extra washing,' she said. 'I can't hear the bell from the scullery. And Captain Reid' – was it my imagination or did her cheeks burn brighter? – 'needs his sheets.'

Let Captain Reid iron his own sheets, I thought.

After Minnie left Miss McKay shook her head. 'It's hard to get staff,' she said. 'A lot of girls have gone to the city to

19

work in munitions. Minnie's no better than she should be. Or would be given half a chance. Smoothing the Captain's sheets indeed!' She shook her head. 'She won't even live in. Goes home every night to a wee huxter of a house up the road with seven brothers and sisters and another on the way.'

I had no idea what a huxter was but clearly it was something to be disapproved of. I couldn't help wondering what Miss McKay would have made of Eupatoria Street.

I remembered that my mother had been *no better than she should be,* and I felt sorry for Minnie. After all *I* was the cause of at least some of the extra laundry, and going home to seven brothers and sisters didn't sound like much fun. But when she came back with the tea Minnie was so smirky that I decided she didn't need my sympathy. I couldn't help admiring her spirit, though: she was just the kind of girl to be useful to the cause. I could imagine her in prison like Rose or fighting with a policeman. Not that there was any need for that these days. The vote had been won. '*Partly* won,' Mam would remind me. 'We don't have the same voting rights as men. It's ridiculous: men can vote at twenty-one; women shouldn't have to wait till they're thirty! Even then, it's not *all* women – only householders or the wives of householders. There's still a great deal to do to change society.' Her eyes would darken, as if she couldn't wait.

But she wasn't around to fight any more, and I was stuck on the edge of a cliff with an old lady, a consumptive widow, an unknown aunt and a pert maid who despised me. I didn't see much chance of changing society.

5

My first thought, when Aunt Nancy bustled in, was shock that she looked so like Mam, though not as pretty: short and solid, with mousy hair pulled into a bun. I'm tall and fair and I'd wondered if I might take after her.

'Stella! You poor thing! Did I get the day wrong?' she cried.

'No. I did.' I stood up, and then wasn't sure if I should kiss or shake hands. Neither seemed right for a stranger who was my only relative.

'You're so …' Nancy shook her head. 'So grown up.' She kept staring, as if she couldn't quite believe I was there. She touched my short hair. 'So fair.'

'Sure the poor cratur mustn't know if she's coming or going,' Miss McKay said. 'Wasn't she marvellous to get here all on her own?'

'You must be exhausted,' Aunt Nancy said. 'Let me take you to your room. I assume that's your bag in the hall? Have you a trunk coming?'

'No. Those are all my worldly goods,' I said brightly.

I followed her upstairs, me carrying my case because I didn't trust it not to splurge its contents everywhere. The walls on the landing were a soft cream, and four white-painted doors led off. Aunt Nancy stopped outside one. 'I've put you in here.'

Both our rooms in Eupatoria Street would have fitted in this room. A huge bay window was crammed with sea and reddening sky. All the furniture was massive and dark, the bed high with a fat chintz eiderdown.

'It's a palace!' I bounced my hands off the eiderdown, which sprang back to full puffiness at once. I felt like Alice in Wonderland when she shrank. I'd never be good enough for this room.

Nancy smoothed the snowy lace-trimmed pillowcase. I wondered if Minnie had ironed it. 'I've always hoped Peggy would come home. Having you is the next best thing.'

'This must be your best room?'

'Yes. It was my parents'. I've never used it. But – well, our parents weren't kind to Peggy when she – when she had her trouble.' She gave a little cough. 'I was only fifteen; I couldn't do anything. I'd like to make it up to you.'

'You could let this room for a decent rent,' I said. 'It's not good business sense to have me in it for free.'

'Business sense! You funny little thing! Now – I'll leave you to make yourself comfortable. There's a bathroom down the passage.'

At Eupatoria Street we shared an outside lavatory with six other tenants, and had to carry every drop of water up from a tap in the yard. Nancy's bathroom was small and chilly, but spotless, with blue flowers printed on the white porcelain lavatory and a strong smell of coal tar soap. The cistern gurgled in a friendly way when I flushed it. All the doors on the first floor were shut, except mine. I heard coughing from behind one and shuddered. An open window at the turn of the stairs overlooked a square back yard and a higgledy-piggledy garden with chickens pecking around making soft *proop proop* noises. Beyond that, black-faced sheep clung to rough steep fields. I heard a door click, and saw Minnie go outside and empty a bucket of water down the drain. She was singing a song I didn't know in a high, clear voice.

The staircase continued up to the attic, and I went to explore. Two doors faced each other on a small windowless landing. One must be Captain Reid's – Sandy's. Funny to be up so many stairs, especially if he had only one leg. Perhaps an attic was all he could afford. I had seen ex-soldiers begging on the streets of Manchester, even officers. Still, living at Cliffside House was hardly destitution, and he had at least one relative who cared about him.

I listened for clues but no noise came from behind either door and I grew tired standing and went back down to my room to unpack. But no matter how I arranged my clothes; my brush and comb; a few books; photos of Mam, including a tiny crumpled snap of her with Rose at a WSPU march; magazine pictures of my heroines, Sylvia Pankhurst and Winifred Carney, who both fought for women's rights – they looked shabby and tiny. The only thing I liked was the view. Standing at the window, unless you looked down, you wouldn't know you were on land: all you could see was sky and sea. A humped grey shadow ran along the horizon – I wasn't sure if it was the Isle of Man or Scotland, but I was comforted by the feeling that my room looked east, back in the direction I had come from.

And when bedtime came, even though I'm tall I had to clamber up on to the bed like a child, and the pillows felt cold and slippery. I was too exhausted not to fall asleep quickly, but I woke a few hours later into a pitch black I'd never experienced – at home there was always a streetlight shining through the curtains – and the mournful crash of the sea smashing against rocks. I stood by the window, seeking some light, and eventually a star pricked the blackness, and then another, until star by star the sky looked friendlier. I'd never seen stars like that in the city.

But it was a long time before I slept again.

6

Life in Cliffside House wasn't remotely as I'd imagined. I'd expected at worst a seaside version of Eupatoria Street, with Aunt Nancy as Mrs Myatt, who had collected rents and handed out post and threatened eviction from her ground-floor lair. Or at best like the Blackpool boarding-house where we'd stayed one August, a skinny, weather-beaten house with rooms chopped in half to make more money.

Nancy called the boarders *guests*. There was no vulgar talk about rents or eviction. You couldn't imagine Miss McKay or wispy Mrs Phillips, who trailed silk scarves and the scent of violets, doing a moonlit flit or fighting drunkenly on the stairs. They ate with Nancy and me in the dining room, and talked to me as if I were about ten, saying what a pity it was there were no other little girls for me to play with.

Captain Reid didn't eat with us. Minnie took his meals up on a tray, and he never seemed to leave his room. I didn't meet him in the queue for the bathroom, or pass him on the stairs, as I did with the others. Perhaps he couldn't walk, but then surely he'd still be in Sunny View or somewhere like it? I hadn't given him the cigarettes. I could have left them outside his room, but I didn't. It was breaking my promise to Helen, but I was waiting for something. I wasn't sure what. There was far too much work for one maid and I felt guilty watching Minnie lug coal buckets and mop floors, but I didn't know how to offer to help: something about her made me feel large and shy.

I couldn't sleep at night and struggled to keep awake by day, my eyes gritty. I read – there were lots of novels in the house, though no political books or pamphlets. There was a set of six Jane Austens with *To Peggy with love from Mama and Papa, Christmas 1899* written inside each in tiny copperplate. Nancy said I could keep them. Miss McKay tried to teach me to knit, but I kept dropping stitches and getting the wool in a tangle. I went for walks, but it was blustery and wet and a wall of grey cloud hung two inches from the end of my nose and never lifted. I looked at the car – a huge Wolseley-Siddeley – and imagined driving far away to somewhere with more action. I couldn't wait to go motoring; I knew I'd love it.

I spent hours looking out the window at the front garden, all windblown and overgrown, drifts of dead leaves getting soggier by the day. I tried not to think about Mam mouldering in the cold earth.

'It's a mess,' Nancy said when she saw me looking. 'Needs a man's touch, but it's impossible with so many men away.'

I couldn't work up much appetite, though the food, considering the war, was good: fresh eggs from Nancy's chickens, and nicer bread than I'd been used to – soda and wheaten, baked on a hot griddle. Nancy did the cooking. In my grandparents' day, she said, there had been a cook and a housekeeper, but there had been more money then, and more people willing to work as servants.

'Are you all right?' she asked me a dozen times a day, and to please her I'd say of course, how could I not be, when she was so kind?

And she *was* kind. 'You're not quite equipped for the east coast of Ireland in winter,' she said diplomatically on the first dry day. 'We'll get you some warm skirts and cardigans and a good coat in Taggart's.'

'In the car?' I felt the first zoom of real pleasure since Mam died.

But it didn't last. Motoring didn't feel modern and racy: it was terrifying. The road seemed to rear up at us. My chest pounded and my stomach swooped. I gripped the dashboard and tried closing my eyes but that was worse. I didn't want Nancy to notice so I made myself stare at the road ahead and try not to gasp with fright, but by the time we were pulling up outside Taggart's Ladies' Outfitters in Main Street my palms were clammy and my legs shook when I got out of the car.

I hardly ever had new clothes, and despite being exhausted, and sad about Mam and feeling upside-downish after the motor ride, I couldn't help thrilling at the prospect. But inside the shop I stared in horror at the dull colours and old-fashioned cuts. Nobody in Manchester still wore skirts to their ankles, not under the age of thirty! And that sailor blouse Nancy made me try – it was like something a *baby* would wear. Sadie and Lil would have wet themselves laughing. Sadie had her hair permed and Lil smoked and had a young man; they had graduated far beyond sailor blouses. 'Um,' I said when the toothy shop assistant pointed out how well made it was. 'Isn't there another shop?'

She sucked her teeth. 'You won't get anything as good as this without going to Belfast. We do favour quality and classic lines here at Taggart's.' She fingered my old skirt. 'Of course, you get what you pay for.'

It was such a waste! Nancy spent pounds and all of it was so frumpy I couldn't look forward to wearing it at all. I remembered Helen's lovely navy coat and a purple and yellow striped cardy Sadie got for her birthday, and sighed as we left the shop.

'I suppose you're used to the latest city fashions,' Nancy said. 'We're behind the times. But that tweed skirt was lovely on you. Miss McKay will turn it up if you want. And it will go with the pink cardigan she's knitting – oh, I don't think you're meant to know that's for you.'

I cheered up then, especially as Nancy said we would go for tea in The Cosy Kettle where she said they had the best scones in the county. 'Peggy used to love them.' She hardly ever talked about Mam so I stored up any little snippets.

But The Cosy Kettle, opposite the bandstand on the front, had its shutters down and a sign in the window: CLOSED DUE TO ILLNESS.

'Oh dear,' Nancy said. My insides twisted the way they always did at any reminder of the flu. We went to the tearoom at the Mountainview Hotel instead, the biggest building in town, which I hoped would be posh inside, but it smelt of fish and pot pourri, and the rock buns were as hard as the harbour wall.

'Nothing's the same since the war,' Nancy said, which is what everyone always said.

I'd expected the war to feel more distant in Cuanbeg: I knew lots of Irish people didn't agree with fighting for Britain, and I remembered the Easter Rebellion of 1916, which had looked very exciting even if it had been doomed. Many of our trade union friends in Manchester had been on the rebels' side. And Winifred Carney, the typist with the revolver who'd been at James Connolly's side in the rebellion, was one of my heroines. But the war was as inescapable here as it was at home. Driving past Sunny View Nancy had said thank goodness the weather had turned so the soldiers could sit out again. Mrs Phillips's husband and two brothers had been killed at the Somme and Miss McKay's twin nephews were fighting. And all over the town, just like in Manchester, people were in mourning. Even when they didn't wear black, you saw it in their faces.

I crumbled my rock cake in my saucer. 'Sorry,' I said. 'I know we shouldn't waste food but honestly, if they had these on the Western Front the war would be over by now.'

She smiled. 'It *must* end soon. Aleppo fell last week. People say that's important. And of course the soldiers are falling like flies from the flu. Germans too, poor beggars.' She lowered her voice when a whiskery, military-looking man at the next table harrumphed disapprovingly. 'I dread it coming to Cliffside House.' She shuddered, and then said, 'Anyway, *you* don't want to be thinking about that, do you?'

I shook my head and stifled a yawn. 'Sorry. I'm not bored, just tired.' *And desperate to change the subject.*

'Of course you're bored,' Nancy said. 'You're a young girl; you're used to the city. Cuanbeg's not at its best this time of year. In the summer you can swim and there are lots of visitors and it's quite lively.'

The summer felt a long way away, and I'd never learned to swim.

'I'm used to having more to do,' I said. 'I did most of the housekeeping because Mam worked such long hours at the munitions and went to so many meetings and that. I thought I'd be coming here to skivvy for you.' I grinned. 'But you already have a skivvy.'

'I don't think Minnie would relish that description.' Nancy poured more tea into my cup. 'So what did you do when you weren't housekeeping? You said you'd left school.'

'I was at the commercial college. Mam didn't want me in a mill or a factory.' She had worked all hours to afford the fees, her hair and skin yellowish from the chemicals. 'You're going to have a better life,' she always said. 'You're the future.'

'Did you like it?' Nancy asked.

I hesitated. I'd liked giggling with Sadie and Lil, and feeling grown-up having occasional sixpenny lunches in town. I enjoyed using the typewriting machine, but hated the shorthand, and though I was looking forward to earning my own money I couldn't see myself tucked away in an office. Probably seen and not heard. If I could be the secretary of a trade union, like Winifred Carney, or of some kind of women's welfare organisation, and change people's lives, that would be different. 'I didn't *hate* it,' I said, 'but it wasn't exactly my dream.'

'So what is your dream?'

To change the world. But that would sound childish. 'I like organising people,' I said. 'And protesting against injustice. In seventh standard I led a strike against the teacher when she said the girls had to knit at breaktime while the boys played outside.'

'Goodness!' Nancy sounded breathless. 'Sounds like you want to be a Member of Parliament.' She laughed, as if suggesting I wanted to be a unicorn.

'Some day women *will* be MPs,' I said. My voice sounded very loud in the stuffy room and the harrumphing colonel or whatever he was tutted and flapped his newspaper with a *crack*.

Nancy looked taken aback. 'You sound very radical.'

'I am. I've been fighting for the vote since I was a kid.' I remembered telling Helen about this; *she* would understand!

'But there's no need for all that any more, is there? I mean, the vote's been won,' Nancy said in a cosy, dismissive voice.

'Not completely. Mam said she wouldn't let her sword sleep in her hand until women could vote on the same terms as men. And *I* won't either.' My voice rang out even clearer now. 'Some of our friends went to *prison* for the cause. Rose Sullivan nearly *died* on hunger strike. I'd do the same if I had to.'

I expected her to say she remembered Rose, but she just twisted her mouth a little and said, 'Hmm. I'd rather you didn't talk about that sort of thing too much in front of Mrs Phillips. Her father was a judge.'

The harrumphing colonel stood up and pushed past us, shaking his head and muttering, 'Little besom. Needs a good spanking.'

I giggled, but Nancy looked worried. 'Oh dear,' she said. 'We'll have to make sure you use up some of that energy. I don't want you restless.'

'Was Mam restless? Is that why …?'

Nancy bit her lip, and looked round the dining room but it was empty now. 'Peggy was so *passionate* about everything. She wanted to go on to Queen's College – Queen's University it is now – but Daddy said he hadn't raised us to be blue-stocking old maids and wouldn't let her. That's when she started going a bit wild.' She gave a sad remembering smile. 'Not what *you'd* call wild. Queen Victoria had only just died. We never had anything like the freedom of you young girls. Daddy wasn't pleased when Peggy chummed up with the Sullivans. *Catholics*,' she said, as if this explained something.

I nodded, hoping she would go on. Mam had only mentioned Rose, nobody else.

'She used to sneak off early in the morning and go swimming in the harbour.'

'That's clearly not all she did,' I dared to say. I hoped Nancy would say something about my father. All Mam would ever say was that he had been killed in an accident years ago. In America. Which I never quite believed.

Nancy blushed. 'I was so jealous of her! I was the plain one, and a bit dull. It didn't seem fair that Peggy should be pretty *and* clever *and* spirited. All *I* had was being the good one. And then, of course – well, she left, so I had to stay. Anyway' – she drained her cup – 'you don't want to hear all this ancient history. Let's go. The sun's out: we'll take a spin round the hills and maybe think of something to stop you being bored.'

She didn't say, *I don't want you going the same way as your mother*, but she didn't have to.

7

A spin round the hills was obviously meant as a treat. I tried to squash my stupid fear. Maybe I just needed to get used to motoring. Maybe it would be easier out on the open road.

It was much worse.

Nancy kept telling me that this part of the coast was famous for its dramatic scenery. It's true that the higher we climbed, the car making alarming dragging noises on some of the bends, the more beautiful the hills were, with the aquamarine sea glinting far below. I tried to look at them. I tried to feel the sharp air blow away my cobwebby restlessness, but the more the car listed and juddered, the more my insides did the same, so that eventually I had to ask Nancy, in a strangled squeak, to stop and let me out. I could hide fear but I couldn't hide being sick, and I wasn't sure which was worse.

'Worse than the boat coming over,' I said after a miserable few minutes in a gateway, my voice thin in the gusting mountain breeze. I breathed in deeply.

'Oh dear.' Nancy patted my arm. 'It's my driving. I don't seem to manage the car as smoothly as Daddy did. Men find that kind of thing easier.'

'Don't say that!' Indignation chased away the remnants of nausea. 'Women drive just as well as men. That's a very reactionary attitude.'

'Maybe,' Nancy said. 'But in my case it's true: I don't drive as well as Daddy.'

I leaned back against the hard metal of the red-painted gate and let the cool air soothe my face. There wasn't much to see, just hills and grass and sheep and three whitewashed farmhouses huddling in hollows. I didn't think I would ever get used to so much space.

'How can people *live* here?' I asked. I'd thought Cliffside House was far from civilisation, but it must be so lonely up on these hills. In a month or two it could be snowing and I imagined they'd be cut off for days.

'It's what they know. The farmers come into town on market days.'

'And the women? The girls?'

'Less often.'

'I'd *die* of boredom.'

Nancy laughed. 'You sound exactly like Peggy. The people up here work too hard to be bored.'

'Do you know them all?'

'Mostly.' She pointed at the farmhouses in turn. 'Agnews; O'Hares; Sullivans –'

My insides flipped in a way that was nothing to do with car-sickness and fear. 'As in *Rose* Sullivan? Mam's friend?'

Nancy nodded, biting her lip.

'We – well, we lost touch.' I didn't want to say there'd been a fight, with shouting and walking out and years of silence. 'You know I'm called after her? Stella *Rose* Graham? She lived with us on and off before the war. When she wasn't in prison.'

'That's her home place,' Nancy said. 'But it's the last place she'd be likely to be. She – apparently became rather wild. Involved in republicanism and trade unions. Worse than the suffragette business. Her parents were mortified. Especially after – well, they'd had enough to –'

'But they'd know where she is? Can't we go and ask? I'd love to make contact with her again!'

'Not now,' Nancy said. 'Maybe when this terrible flu's over.' That was like saying never. 'Now, let's go home.'

'Will you drive slowly?' My voice sounded small and worried.

I wasn't sick on the way home, but, oh, it was deadly, crawling along at five miles an hour, and wincing when the gears crashed. I tried to calm myself by watching what Nancy's feet and hands were doing; it didn't look very difficult. Maybe I wouldn't be so terrified if I was in control. Being scared was *not* how I wanted to see myself.

'*I* could learn to drive,' I suggested, as we were coming down the steep back road behind Cliffside House, past the rough-walled cottage where Minnie lived. A line of grey, patched washing stretched from gatepost to tree. 'I could do your shopping and – well, whatever you needed.' *And explore. And find a proper town with a picture house and girls to talk to and laugh with. And look for Rose. Surely her family can tell me where she is. If she is alive or dead.*

Nancy shook her head. 'You're too young. And it's a big, heavy car.'

'I'm strong. I like difficult things.'

Nancy turned the car into the loaning, so sharply that I had to grab at my hat. 'It's out of the question, at least for a year or so.' She drew the car to a ragged halt in front of the house. *A year or so …* Sighing, I opened my door and stepped out, my legs wobbly to find themselves back on firm ground.

Nancy looked up at the attic windows and frowned. I followed her glance and saw, as I had the first day, the outline of someone – a man – standing at the window looking out to sea.

'I wish Captain Reid would go out and get some air,' she said. 'There won't be many more days like this when winter comes, and the exercise would help him.'

'Why does he live here?' I asked.

'For the peace and quiet. Understandable after the Western Front. Doesn't want to go back to the city.' I waited for her to say more, but she didn't.

I'd swap the city for here any day, I felt like saying, but then Nancy bent and lifted the boxes and parcels from Taggart's out of the car, and I felt guilty.

Instead I looked at the neglected garden. Presumably if Captain Reid had enough limbs for exercise, he would be capable of doing some weeding and raking. 'Pity *he* doesn't help in the garden,' I said.

Nancy sighed. 'He's a paying guest; it's not his job.'

'You said it needs a man's hand. He's the only man around.'

'Maybe that was – what did you call it? – *reactionary* of me. What's wrong with the garden having a woman's hand?' She raised her eyebrows in a challenge. 'Or a girl's?'

'*I* know nothing about gardening!'

'You could rake up the leaves and tidy the shrubs. It's like housework, only outdoors.' She turned to walk up the steps to the front door, balancing the parcels across her arms. 'You don't have to, Stella – but if you really do like difficult things …'

I tilted my chin. 'Certainly,' I said. 'I'll start straight away.'

8

Bending, stooping, raking, sweating. I didn't think a ten-hour shift in a munitions factory could be as exhausting as this.

I balled my fists into the small of my back, like I'd seen Mam do after a long day. I spat out a wet leaf that had somehow got into my mouth, then bent over the rake again, pulling the soggy brown hump of leaves along. I kept thinking somebody was watching me, but every time I looked up the house stared blankly back.

I liked seeing the lawn emerge, green and neat, from under the drifts of leaves. I even quite liked the pain and sweat, knowing that I would be able to have a lovely warm bath in a proper bathroom afterwards. I was so hot I'd taken off my coat, and then my brown cardigan, and hung them over a shrub. I felt like a Land Girl, a noble daughter of the soil, and though the work was tedious, I no longer felt bored and restless. And for the first time I was looking forward to my tea.

'What are you doing?'

I looked up to see Minnie, her skirt peeping under a shabby tweed coat that barely reached her knees.

What d'you think I'm doing? is what I'd have said to Sadie or Lil. 'Tidying up.'

She sniffed. 'They'll get blew everywhere.' Sure enough the wind was already starting to tease at my huge leaf-pile, making it whiffle and scatter. 'The compost heap's down at the bottom,' she went on. 'Behind yon rhododendron. You'd've been better to have raked them in that direction.'

'I know what I'm doing,' I lied. Blast and damnation! Why hadn't I thought to check where the compost heap was? 'Is it six o'clock already?' I asked, looking up at the sky which was fading but not yet dusky. Minnie usually left at six.

'Ma's been took bad. She's near her time. I'll have to keep the wee ones out of the road.' She sighed. 'I hope she's not at it all night like she was with our Sammy.' Her shoulders drooped as she walked off, looking both older and younger than the pert girl I'd met the day I arrived.

The only way to get the leaves to the compost heap was to lift great piles and stagger down the hill with them. This involved several journeys, a lot of swearing, even more sweat, and getting my hands slimy with dirt. Only when I took the rake back to the shed in the yard did I see the wheelbarrow that would have made life easier. By the time I got back to the house I'd had enough of gardening for ever, but when Nancy said I looked tired, I found myself promising to tackle the weed-choked borders next day.

Properly dirty and aching, I appreciated the bathroom

more than ever, stretching out my stiff legs in the scented water and soaping myself all over. I wondered who was using our old tin bath at Eupatoria Street.

The dinner bell was clanging as I left the bathroom, glowing and damp and smelling of Nancy's lemon verbena bath salts rather than sweat, so I didn't wait to dress, but went down in my camel dressing gown. Nancy, who I met at the dining room door, carrying a large dish of rabbit pie, frowned.

'I'd hoped you could take Captain Reid's tray up to him, since Minnie's had to go early.'

'Of course I can.'

'Not in your dressing gown!'

I looked down at myself. 'I'm perfectly decent,' I said. 'It covers more of me than any of my frocks.' I felt suddenly no better than I should be, and my lovely dressing gown, Mam's last birthday present, indecent and slatternly.

'No, I'll take it. You go on in and sit down.'

'It would be easier for you if he came to meals like everyone else,' I said idly. 'Women shouldn't have to wait on men.'

'It would be even easier for me,' Nancy said, her tone as sharp as the gamey smell of the rabbit, 'if you didn't see fit to express opinions about things you have no understanding of.'

I felt like she'd hit me. I opened my mouth to argue and then, for once in my life, shut it again.

9

I met Captain Reid next morning. Minnie didn't appear, and Nancy asked me to take up his breakfast tray. 'Just knock and leave it at the door,' she said.

I knew she meant outside the door – there was a little table there which I guessed was for that purpose. Maybe it had been placed there to deter the lovelorn Minnie. But I wouldn't be so easily daunted. I knocked, said, 'Breakfast!' and pushed open the door, careful not to tilt the tray with its bowl of porridge and pot of tea under a bright orange knitted cosy.

What if he's in bed? What if he's in a state of undress? I thought, but it was too late to back out.

A fug of smoke and stale sleepy air made me cough.

'Minnie?' The voice was deep, male, surprised.

'Um, no. It's Stella.'

Through the smoke haze I saw him standing by the window with his back to me. Tall, red-haired, dressed, not, as I'd stupidly imagined, in army uniform, but in a navy jersey and flannels. He had all his limbs. He turned and said, 'The little gardener?'

I dumped the tray on a table in the middle of the room. So he had been watching. He was watching me now, in a disconcerting, creepy way – one eye slid past me.

'I'm not actually the gardener.' I ignored the insulting *little*.

'That was obvious.' He barely took the cigarette out of his mouth to speak. Sarcastic beast.

'I'm Nancy's niece. I live here. She doesn't have time for the garden, she's so busy, so I was helping her.' I emphasised the *helping*.

'Is there anything else?' he asked, which should have been my line, if I'd really been the maid.

'No,' I said. And then I remembered that I liked difficulty and challenge. 'Just – well, I'll be gardening again today. And it's heavy work.' Some girls would have added, *for a girl*, to appeal to his sense of chivalry, but of course *I* wouldn't stoop so low. 'Just in case you felt like some fresh air.' I coughed again, to emphasise how fuggish it was in here. Clearly, he was managing to get cigarettes without the packet Helen had brought.

'I don't,' he said, stubbing his cigarette end into a glass ashtray. 'Another time, just leave the tray outside.'

'Certainly.' My voice was clipped, and I tilted my chin so high as I walked to the door that I could hardly see where I was going.

If *that* was a war hero, I wasn't impressed. If *that* was an officer and a gentleman I didn't think much of his manners.

All day long I took my annoyance out on the weeds I was piling up for a bonfire. It was extremely satisfying, pretending they were Captain Reid. *He's awfully nice,* Helen had said. I hadn't believed her then and I certainly didn't believe her now.

Minnie didn't turn up all day. I tried – ugh – not to think of her poor mother giving birth, but every so often my thoughts wandered away from the garden, down the loaning, and up the stony road to that mean cottage. I didn't see how they could fit in one extra person, even a tiny baby.

Nancy, back from her weekly stint at Sunny View, came to see how I was getting on. I yanked at something spindly and brown. '*Is* this a weed?' I rubbed my aching hand on my skirt.

Nancy stroked one of the feathery leaves. 'It doesn't *look* very nice, but everything's been neglected since Mama died. It might be an exquisite rare bloom for all I know.'

'It might have to stay where it is,' I admitted. 'It's too strong for me to pull out.'

'When the war's over, I'll see if I can get a man to do the heavy work,' she said. I didn't mention my sour exchange with Captain Reid.

'Anyway,' Nancy went on, her tone changing, 'I want to ask you something. I've been asked to take another boarder. A new VAD nurse from Sunny View. It's been hard to get billets in the town because so many households have the flu.' She touched the bare twig of a shrub. People often touched wood when they mentioned the flu.

'Brilliant!' A nurse would be young and lively and modern; the very thought of it perked me up so much I gave the weed/precious rare bloom an extra hard tug and it gave up the ghost and yielded.

'I've only the attic left. And it's very small. She could have my room, but –'

'No! Give her my room. Honestly, Nancy, I'd love to sleep in the attic.'

She laughed. 'Well, I'd like to be able to help. Matron's a good sort.'

'And it's a good contact, isn't it? There'll be a steady stream of nurses needing rooms.'

'Not if the war ends like everyone says it's going to.'

I thought of all those wheeled chairs parked on Sunny View's veranda. Even if the war did end soon, it wouldn't really be *over*.

10

Miss Catherine Reilly was to move in on Sunday 3 November. It took me three minutes to clear out of my room on Saturday, and about four to arrange my things in the small attic. It had a low, sloped ceiling but a proper window overlooking the hills at the back of the house. There was a dressing table, a built-in cupboard, a small iron bedstead, and a dear little corner fireplace. I put my pictures on the mantelshelf, along with the six red-bound Jane Austens which looked very cheerful against the faded floral wallpaper.

I didn't stop to admire my new abode, though: there was too much to do. I couldn't help being pleased that Minnie hadn't reappeared, even though it meant trailing up to the attic every mealtime with Captain Reid's tray. My new bedroom was opposite the horrible Captain's. Still, I needn't have anything to do with him. As long as I couldn't smell his revolting smoke or hear him snoring, I could pretend he wasn't there.

I wanted Miss Reilly's room to be perfect. I fetched the best sheets from the linen cupboard, and chose the crispest pillowcases, snowy and lavender-scented.

'You're a darling,' Nancy said, when she came into the room with a little vase of rust-coloured chrysanthemums and found me plumping up the eiderdown. She looked round the gleaming room, all the woodwork shining. I'd helped keep things clean in Eupatoria Street, but the furniture there didn't *glow*. 'Look,' she went on, placing the vase on the mantelshelf. 'These had been completely hidden by weeds until you tidied up.'

'Lovely.' I set them on the chest of drawers where they looked cheerful and welcoming. My heart skipped. Would Miss Reilly let me call her Catherine? Maybe she'd be Cathy or Kitty or Kate? Whatever I called her, I imagined us drinking cocoa in our dressing gowns like the college girls I'd read about, talking into the night.

On Sunday morning I sat down for breakfast as usual, my heart singing at the thought of a new friend.

Nancy raised her eyebrows at my old frock. 'You can't garden on a Sunday!'

'Why not? You don't go to church.' I knew the Irish were famously God-bothering and I'd been relieved, last Sunday, that nobody in Cliffside House had gone to church.

'We do, usually,' Nancy said. 'We've missed a few weeks because of the flu. They're advising people against crowded places.'

'Though surely this is a time when we need to go to church more than ever.' Miss McKay looked worried.

'After all, many people believe this plague has been sent to punish us.' She spread marmalade on her toast and sighed.

'I'm sure God wouldn't expect us to put ourselves at risk.' Mrs Phillips gave one of her little dry coughs. 'I had a letter from the Reverend Mehaffey – my minister at home – saying his time is nearly all taken up with funerals this last while.' She tutted. 'There are babies waiting to be christened and he's had to turn them away.'

I concentrated on spooning up my porridge, willing the conversation to take a less morbid turn. Talking about God was weird – Mam hadn't brought me up in any faith, though I gathered her family were Protestants – but at least it wasn't painful. But flu – ugh. Especially when people started talking about it being a plague and a judgement.

Mam's face, nearly black as the cyanosis spread across from her blueing lips. My own voice, sobbing: This can't be just flu!

'I respect your beliefs,' I said in a voice loud enough to drown out the memory, 'but I'm not a believer myself.' Mrs Phillips choked on her toast. 'So I *will* be working in the garden this morning.'

11

I was washing the day's grime off in the bathroom when Miss Reilly arrived. I hadn't bothered going all the way upstairs to fetch my dressing gown, and had just stripped off to my camisole and drawers. I heard the doorbell, and voices, and feet on the stairs. Damn! I dropped the soap and had to scrabble for it under the basin. *I* had meant to be the one to welcome her.

Nancy rattled the door handle. 'Occupied,' I heard her say. 'Well – this is the bathroom. You'll have to take my word for it.'

I sat down on the lavatory seat and tried to breathe quietly. I couldn't leave now. I didn't want them thinking I'd been on the lav, and I couldn't bear them to see me in my greying, patched underwear, which made me look about twelve. Neither could I put my frock back on; I had knelt in something unspeakable – fox dirt, I thought, and the smell was disgusting. In fact, though I'd rolled my frock into a ball, I suspected the bathroom would still stink after I left. Catherine was bound to need the lavatory after her journey. She would pounce the moment the door clicked, see me rushing upstairs in my shabby underwear, smell the awful smell and think it was me. My face burned.

'I'll leave you to settle in,' Nancy said. 'Dinner's at seven but I'll bring you some tea to keep you going.'

I heard her go downstairs and waited to hear the bedroom door close so I could escape. But it didn't – Catherine probably didn't want to miss the exact moment when the bathroom became free. In the end I just grabbed my rolled-up frock, turned the key as silently as I could, opened the door and dashed upstairs. With luck she would think the bathroom hogger/stinker was Captain Reid or Mrs Phillips – anyone but me.

In the attic I looked at my reflection in the slightly spotty glass. Miss McKay had been right: I did have rosy cheeks now. But did they make me look too young? I brushed my hair and felt better: my bob was definitely sophisticated and ageing. I changed into my new tweed skirt, with one of the blouses Mam had bought me for college, a green candy-stripe with a square collar. It was a little tight which made my bosom stick out in a very gratifying way. I bit down hard on my lips to make them redder.

I went downstairs before seven to collect Captain Reid's tray from the kitchen.

'Good girl,' Nancy said. 'You look very smart.' She indicated the tray on the table. 'There you go. Hopefully you won't have to keep doing that.'

'Why? Is he leaving? Or is Minnie coming back?'

Nancy shook her head. 'I'm hoping the presence of a

pretty young woman might lure Captain Reid out of his lair. After all, they're about the same age.'

No! Catherine's going to be my *friend!* I frowned at the plate. I wasn't sure which offended me more – the idea of Reid stealing my new friend or Nancy's assumption that *I* wasn't pretty enough to lure him out. And I was angry at myself for even thinking that.

'He's *years* older than her,' I said, though actually I didn't know what age Catherine was.

'He's twenty-two.'

'He doesn't *look* twenty-two.'

'Take that food while it's hot. If you'd spent the best part of four years fighting on the Western Front, you'd look older too,' Nancy said.

'*I'm* a pacifist,' I said, as I backed out of the room.

'Not on the home front you aren't,' Nancy retorted. 'Ring the gong on the way past.'

When I got to the dining room, Nancy wasn't there and a young woman sat beside Miss McKay. She nodded at me but seemed intent on helping herself to potatoes.

'Miss Graham was called to the door,' Mrs Phillips said. 'She told us to go ahead.'

'And this is the baby of our wee household,' Miss McKay said. 'Miss Graham's niece, Stella. Stella – Miss Catherine Reilly.'

'Kit,' she said. She was medium height and dark-haired and, to my disappointment, not in uniform. She ate with enthusiasm.

'Lovely rissoles,' Miss McKay said, and looked approving

when I tucked in. 'See – you're working up an appetite out in yon garden. I'll be soon having to take that skirt out as well as up.'

'And she's got roses in her cheeks,' Mrs Phillips added, as if I was about four.

'Didn't I say she would?'

I looked at the big jug of chrysanthemums on the sideboard and sighed. Just then Nancy returned, her brow creased.

'What is it?' I asked.

'I'm afraid we'll have to keep on doing without Minnie,' she said. 'That was her little sister.'

Mrs Phillips looked round us all, and, perhaps deciding that as the only married woman in the house she was the proper person to broach the indelicate subject of childbirth, said, 'Surely her mother's been delivered by now?'

'She's had the baby – a boy; but now she has the flu.'

'Oh!' Mrs Phillips drew back a little, as if Nancy could have caught the disease from the child at the door. Kit helped herself to more potatoes.

'Is there anyone to help them?' Miss McKay asked.

'Only Minnie,' Nancy said. 'I wonder if we should –'

Mrs Phillips moaned, and pressed her napkin to her mouth. 'Oh no! Miss Graham, I implore you – we *must* keep well away.'

'Minnie's only fifteen.' Nancy explained that Minnie was our maid, and lived about half a mile up the road. 'There's a father,' she said, 'but I can't imagine he'll be much help. It doesn't seem very neighbourly not to …'

I stared at my plate, and the rissole which had been so plump and appetising looked greasy and solid. No neighbours had come near us when Mam was ill. They were sick themselves, or scared. I heard again Mam's bubbling cough, saw the blood frothing at her mouth, smelt – oh God! I swallowed and laid my knife and fork down. *Don't ask me to go,* I begged inside my head. I'd had flu; I was probably safe not to get it again. Hadn't I said I wanted something hard to do? But not that.

'This is no time to be neighbourly,' Mrs Phillips said. 'You have this whole household to think of.'

'What do *you* think? As a professional?' Nancy turned to Kit, her face anxious.

'Actually, nothing does much good,' she said. Then, as if wanting to please, added, 'If you've whiskey in the house, it seems to help as much as anything.'

'There's a little left over from my father's time,' Nancy said. 'For medicinal purposes. I could take a bottle to the Mahons tomorrow, maybe. Just leave it at the gate.'

Mrs Phillips patted Miss Reilly's hand. Her heavy rings glittered on her long thin fingers. 'It'll be a great comfort to have a medical professional in the house,' she said. '*I* suffer badly with my chest, as you've probably noticed. *I* daren't risk influenza. But if I should succumb – well, they say nursing is the one thing that makes the difference.'

Kit looked at Mrs Phillips as if she would rather stab her than nurse her. 'It's the young and fit who seem to be struck down hardest,' she said. 'You'll probably be grand.' And she turned away to ask Miss McKay something.

'Now, we *don't* want our new guest thinking we'd take advantage of her expertise,' Nancy said with a frown. 'This house should be a sanctuary for Kit, away from all the – well, the unpleasantness. Though Sunny View is a very happy place. In its way.' She started to talk about Matron, how kind she was, and how staunchly the town supported the home, raising money for comforts and getting up concerts for the patients. How brave and splendid the men were.

Mam was brave and splendid. I remembered being with her and Rose at a WSPU rally, shouting 'Votes for Women!' I'd held one of her hands, while she held the end of a banner with the other. I'd been puffed with pride, hoping someone from school would see me. Mam and Rose shouted louder than anyone. Rose had been arrested for hitting a policeman; Mam never did anything like that because of me. That was Rose's first time in prison.

'Let's hope the disease does not infiltrate Sunny View.' Miss McKay's voice brought me back to the present. 'Those poor wounded heroes have suffered enough.'

'They had it in the early summer,' Nancy said, 'but mildly. Nobody died.' She smiled round the table in what was clearly meant to be a reassuring way.

'It blazed through St Anne's – my last place – like a dose of salts,' Kit said. 'At one point I was the only nurse for thirty men, all coughing and vomiting and screaming. Writhing in their own filth. Turning blue and dying. I've been a VAD for two years but this was like – I don't know, some medieval pestilence.'

My breath shuddered. *Make her stop*!

Kit forked up some parsnip purée. 'This is jolly good.'

Mrs Phillips drew her scarf tighter round her neck, as if protecting herself from the disease half a mile away. 'It's a judgement. It has to be. Mankind has gone mad – all this killing – and the Lord has sent his vengeance.'

Writhing. Turning blue. Dying.

'The war *may* have something to do with it,' Kit said. 'All those men holed up together in stinking trenches. They say the rats are as big as cats, and all those bodies lying unburied –'

Miss McKay put her hand on Kit's arm. '*Pas devant l'enfant*,' she murmured. 'She's gone a wee bit green. And who can blame her.'

'Sorry, kiddie.' For the first time Kit seemed to notice me. 'I've a wee sister your age. She's pretty squeamish too. Fainted when the cat had kittens in the airing cupboard.' She laughed.

My rissoles blurred and swam in a film of tears. *They say nursing is the one thing that makes the difference.*

I did my best, Mam. I did everything I could. But it wasn't enough.

A solid ball of tears rose in my throat.

'Excuse me,' I managed to choke out, and throwing my napkin down I ran out of the room, up the stairs, up and up.

'Oh!' I hadn't seen Captain Reid until I was nearly on top of him. He must have been putting his tray back on the table outside his room. He shrank back into his doorway. His eyes looked past me in that weird way.

I shoved past him into the sanctuary of my room. I slammed the door shut and flung myself onto the bed, where I sobbed like the baby they all thought I was.

12

I jerked awake into shrieking dark. I sat up in confusion. My skirt was all bunched round my middle, and my face was sticky. For a moment I thought I'd woken myself crying, as I'd done so often just after Mam died.

But another scream tore through the night, and I realised it came from next door. I lit my candle and rushed out of the room. Outside Captain Reid's door I hesitated. It was quiet now. Maybe I should mind my own business. Then I remembered how I'd lain awake those last disturbed nights in Manchester, shaking, longing for someone – anyone – to come and be with me, and I pushed the door open. The room smelt of smoke and sweat and a sharp acrid smell I couldn't identify.

My candle flickered. Captain Reid wasn't lying in bed shaking and grateful for human comfort. He was standing at the side of the bed, dragging the sheets off. He turned and they landed with a flump.

'What do you want?' he asked.

'I'm sorry – I heard – I thought you were having a nightmare.'

'I'm fine,' he said. 'As you can see.' He was wearing only pyjama trousers and a vest; the candlelight turned his shoulders gold but revealed a network of jagged red scars marching down one arm. It also showed that his sheets were wet, and I knew what the smell was. I had a sudden memory of Minnie, laundering extra sheets for Captain Reid on my first day.

'Can I help? I know where the clean sheets are kept.'

'No, thank you. It's all under control.'

'It's no bother –'

'I said *no*!' He sat down hard on the bed and fumbled on the bedside table. His hands shook so much he knocked the cigarette packet on to the floor. I picked it up and handed to him. He opened it and said, 'Damn. Run out of smokes.' He looked lost.

'Hold on.'

I dashed back to my room and came back with the packet Helen had left with me. Gallahers Blues, the same as the empty packet. I didn't explain where they'd come from and he showed no curiosity. Maybe he thought I was the kind of girl who kept cigarettes in her room. Maybe, as an officer and a gentleman, he was used to having minions appearing with whatever he needed.

Or, I thought, as he shoved a cigarette in his mouth, lit it with a shuddering match and sucked on it as gratefully as I'd gasped in the clean mountain air after being car-sick, he was just desperate for a smoke.

And he did say thank you, but in a tone that also meant, *Go away.*

13

I looked up from weeding the rose-bed to see Captain Reid, hands dug into the pockets of a dark overcoat, face shadowed by a tweed cap. I dug my fork into the earth; it was harder today, after the first frost of the year. He didn't say anything. When he took out a cigarette case and lit up, his hands shook nearly as badly as they had last night. I wondered how long it had been since he was last outside.

'Have you come to help?' I asked. I wasn't sure how damaged his arm was, but I bet it could wield a fork or help push a wheelbarrow.

'I came to ask you not to …' He sucked on his cigarette and looked away.

Up close, his skin was reddened by the sharp wintry air, and one eye watered. I realised why I had found his gaze so disconcerting: his left eye was squint and blind, the iris milky like an old dog's. He shivered in his big coat, and I didn't know if it was cold or something else.

'I won't tell anyone about last night,' I said, 'if that's what you're worried about. I wouldn't dream of it. Sorry – that wasn't meant to be a pun.'

His lips twitched. 'Thanks. Just – you know.' He gestured back at the house.

'Fancy helping? You can weed, or prune. I've got to cut all these bushes back so they can't get destroyed by the wind.'

He hesitated.

'It'll warm you up.' I held out my fork. 'And – well, I started sleeping better after I started working in the garden. Maybe …'

He stubbed out his half-smoked cigarette on the trunk of a tree and took the fork. I took secateurs and began to prune the rosebushes. They looked horrible – naked thorny stalks; impossible to imagine them coming back as fat green bushes full of flowers next summer, but Nancy said that was what needed doing, so I was doing it.

We worked side by side. He didn't say another word apart from 'Is that a weed?' and fled indoors the moment he saw Kit cycling up the path in her uniform. I didn't admire Captain Reid or anything soppy like that, but I couldn't help smiling to think that, far from being lured by the charms of the pretty nurse, he had scarpered as soon as he'd seen her.

Kit jumped off her bicycle and nodded at me. 'All right, kiddie?' she asked. 'Gardening's a super hobby.'

'I'm not a *kiddie*,' I said. 'And I hate gardening. But there's nobody else.' I looked at her bicycle, black and gleaming, a little muddy round the wheels, a couple of leaves caught in the front spokes. I reached out and touched the handlebar closest to me; it felt solid and full of promise.

'There's no need to be so fierce,' she said. 'I'm only trying to be friendly.'

I thought of how much I wanted her to see me as an equal. I imagined us cycling down the hill into the town and beyond, bright woollen scarves floating behind us in the wind. I don't know where I imagined my cycle would come from. Or maybe she would lend me her bicycle and I could ride up to Rose Sullivan's home place. I felt a little frisson at the idea. Even an address for Rose that I could write to, to tell her Mam was dead, would be something.

'Sorry,' I said. 'But you seem to think I'm an infant.'

'What age are you?'

'Nearly sixteen. The same age my mother was when she had *me*. Out of wedlock.' I added this to shock her. To make me sound quite the woman of the world.

Kit opened and closed her mouth like a goldfish and said, 'Gosh. You're very frank.'

I smiled at the heap of thorny branches in my wheelbarrow. 'Well, I'm a modern girl.'

14

Sandy – I had stopped thinking of him as Captain Reid – came out to the garden every day. He didn't say much, and he always seemed uneasy, huddling into his overcoat, but he took whatever tool I gave him – fork or rake – and did what I asked. Like me, he knew nothing about gardening.

'We only have a tiny garden in Belfast. Terraced house.'

'I thought you officers were all posh. Ancestral acres.'

'My father was a clerk in a shipping office.'

'That's posh where I come from.'

I told him a potted version of my life story, leaving out the finer details of being illegitimate. I didn't want him to assume, as Nancy seemed to be afraid, that I was like my mother, that I was in some way setting my cap at him because I was no better than I should be. I didn't feel romantic about him; he was too old, and too quiet, and I wasn't soppy about men anyway; I'd much rather have a pal. I kept wishing he'd mention Helen but he never did.

Kit was very busy at Sunny View, and days went by

without me catching more than the tantalising whir of bicycle wheels on the gravel of the driveway.

The garden looked much better. Fresh leaves came down every time it was stormy – which, on the east coast of Ulster in November, was often – but I raked them up regularly. The roses, pruned down to twigs, looked raw and vulnerable, but today's job was to put a mulch of leaves round them for protection. Nancy said her mother had always got straw from the Mahons but leaves would have to do this year.

'We should plant bulbs for spring,' I said.

Sandy looked doubtful. 'How d'you know there aren't some under there already?'

'I don't. But so far all we've done is cut things down. It would be nice to plant something and wait for it to grow. Sort of hopeful. Like having a stake in the future.' I thought of a bed of crocuses like stars, opening one by one on a February morning.

Sandy sheltered his cigarette from the east wind. 'Feels like it's been winter for ever.'

'Well, it hasn't. It's only the seventh of November. We could go into town and buy snowdrops and crocuses and' – I tried to remember what had been in the parks at home – 'daffodils. There's a hardware shop that sells gardening things. Unless it's closed,' I added, because you couldn't take it for granted, these days, that any business would be open from one day to the next. This week the laundry had been late back, and the butcher hadn't delivered.

Sandy shook his head. 'It's too far.'

'There's nothing wrong with your legs, is there? It's not *that* far. *I've* walked it,' I said. And without thinking too much I went on, 'And so's Helen.'

The air seemed to freeze. '*What?*' Sandy asked, and there was nothing I could do but blunder on.

'Your cousin Helen? I met her the day I came. She was leaving as I arrived. That's actually where I got the cigarettes I gave you the night – um, the night –'

'And what did she say?' His voice was cold.

'Only that you wouldn't see her.' I patted some leaves tightly round a stem, breaking off to swear and suck my finger when I stuck it into a thorn. 'Ouch! *And* she said you were awfully nice,' I added, in case this helped.

It didn't.

'I came here so I *wouldn't* have a lot of women gossiping about me.' Sandy flung down his fork and stalked off back to the house.

'No wonder she said she wouldn't come back!' I called after him. He kicked the wheelbarrow. I hoped it hurt. 'Temper!' I shouted, which is what Mam used to say when I had tantrums as a kid.

Nancy, turning a sheet sides-to-middle in the sitting room, said she couldn't remember what spring bulbs had or hadn't been planted in the past. 'But I've no objection to you planting more,' she said. 'It's lovely to see you taking an interest. And I see Captain Reid's been helping. That's a miracle! I don't think he's left his room in the three months he's been here, apart from to go to the bathroom.' And she looked down at the sheet and blushed, maybe at the mention of men and bathrooms. She wouldn't have lasted a day in Eupatoria Street.

'Can I go into town now?' I asked. 'Then I can plant them tomorrow.'

Nancy's face clouded. 'Alone?'

'I don't need a *chaperone*! I used to get two trams to college every day! I won't talk to strange men.'

'It's not so much that. It's all this flu –'

'I won't let anyone breathe on me. I'll go straight into the shop and out again, and I'll keep my scarf up round my mouth and nose. I'll be so careful. But I could get some shopping. You were saying the butcher hadn't called.'

'That's right. The delivery boy must be ill. Unless the butcher's actually closed; he might be … Oh, I wonder if I should take you?'

No! I thought. My insides squirmed. *Not the car!* Then a worse fear gripped me when Nancy sighed and went on, 'But I'm really not feeling quite – and this is the first time I've sat down all day.'

'You're not ill, are you?' I searched her face in alarm, and saw that she was paler than usual.

'Just – well, my monthly trouble. I sometimes feel a wee bit sore.' She looked down at her sewing.

'Me too!' Relief made me eager. 'Mam used to give me a hot water bottle to put on my tummy. I'll run and get you one!'

She shook her head. 'When I was your age I wouldn't have mentioned such a thing.'

I shrugged. 'Mam said it was hard enough being a girl

without all the secrecy.' When I'd started my monthlies she'd explained what it was, and given me some soft linen rags for the flow and told me it was private, but not shameful. 'If *I'd* known more when I was your age …' she'd said. 'But then I wouldn't have had you.' And, annoyingly, hadn't said any more.

I didn't tell Nancy any of that; I just repeated that I'd be careful and in the end she let me go, and gave me money and a basket. 'It would be *much* easier if I had a bicycle,' I hinted.

'Well, Christmas is coming,' she said. 'You never know …'

'It would be the best thing to happen to me *ever*.'

'It would have to be second-hand.'

'*That* wouldn't matter.' Excitement bubbled in me. 'Just something to get around on. And when I get a job it'll make life easier.'

She raised her eyebrows. 'You don't need a job. I'm very happy to keep you. It's the least –'

'I don't want to be *kept*.'

'It's what girls do, love.'

'Not girls like me. It's 1918! The world's changed. Women are getting the vote. Not enough women, and not before time, but still – things *will* get better, and I want to be part of it. *I'm* not going to sit round waiting for some man.'

'So what *do* you want?'

But this was where I stuck. I was grateful Mam hadn't let me go into a mill; but I didn't want to go to the city alone, eking out twopences for the gas meter and typing all day in a stuffy office. Mam may have dreamed of Queen's College, but I hadn't had enough schooling, and anyway, though I'd enjoy living with other girls and having cocoa parties like the girls in books, I wasn't that keen on actual *studying*. I thought of my heroine, Winifred Carney – she'd been one of the first Irish women to qualify as a secretary, but she'd ended up being part of a revolution. That's what I'd like. Something dramatic. Something to change the world.

'I don't know,' I said. 'And I know there's plenty for me to do here right now. But when the war ends – when the flu ends – things'll change.'

'It feels like tempting fate to say *when*,' Nancy said. 'Now' – her tone changed – 'off you go, or it'll be dusk before you get home. And be careful!'

The town was even deader than on the day I'd arrived. The few people I saw were muffled in scarves. In the churchyard beside the Catholic church in Main Street, a small knot of people stood around an open grave, intoning what sounded like a prayer. The memory of Mam's funeral stabbed me and I hurried past.

The hardware store was open, and the old man there seemed glad of a customer, and kept me talking for ages about spring colour, and making sure to plant the bulbs the right way up. He slipped an extra packet of snowdrop bulbs into my basket for free. 'Sure it's a wee bit of hope, isn't it?' he said.

The butcher's was closed, blinds pulled down over the door and window. I looked at the windows over the shop, and imagined I could hear someone crying, but it was probably just the whine of the sea breeze. All the same I rushed past. There was a shuffling queue outside the chemist's and a notice in the window read: PLEASE BE ADVISED – NO QUININE LEFT.

A sign outside the newsagents read FLU RAGES IN BELFAST JAIL! and I decided to buy a paper. At home, Mam and I had gone regularly to the Ladies' Reading Room, but the last time I'd even tried to read a paper was the *Belfast Telegraph* on the train on the way down here.

Leaning against the wall outside the shop – 'like a corner boy!' I imagined Mrs Phillips saying – I shivered at the news. There was lots about the war ending – *When the boys come home* – but on the same page there was an article about the latest recruiting figures. And the flu. Always the flu. Trams were being sprayed with disinfectant; schools were closed; hospitals were bursting. Maybe it really was the end of the world.

I imagined, in other streets, in England, in France, in America and Canada and Australia, even in Africa, though I wasn't sure if they had streets and newspapers there, other girls leaning against other walls, reading the same horrible news, wondering if they would be next. The French for flu was *la grippe*. I remembered Miss Braithwaite teaching us that it was pronounced *greep*, not *grip*, but now I thought, remembering the way Mam had writhed and screamed and turned blue, that *grip* was right: it was like she had been seized by an evil power.

Across the street, a child coughed and its mother shushed it. For a second I saw myself from the outside, a lonely girl leaning against a cold wall, with a dying and diseased world spinning round her. The sea air tasted fresh and clean but who knew what it carried?

Oh, for crying out loud! This trip was meant to cheer me up. Now, what could I do to make friends with Sandy? I went back into the shop and looked at the sweets. There was proper seaside rock, with *A present from Cuanbeg* printed on it, but it looked like it had been there since before the war. I bought a bar of Fry's chocolate cream. I liked that better, and if he spurned my peace-offering at least I could eat it myself.

15

I slipped the chocolate under Sandy's door, wrapped in a sheet of notepaper where I'd scribbled, 'A present from the outside world.' A few minutes later he knocked on my door. He held out the bar and at first I thought he was refusing it, but he said, 'Share?'

I pulled the door open wide. 'Come in,' I said. 'I've bought a paper. You can read it before I give it to Nancy.' I gestured at the *Telegraph* on the bed, hoping he would be impressed by my interest in world affairs, but he shook his head.

'We could go for a walk?' I suggested.

His good eye narrowed as if I'd said something wrong, and he crossed to the window, which was already greying with dusk.

'See?' he said. 'It's too dark.'

'I don't mind the dark.' I stood beside him and looked at the sky. 'First one to spot a star gets extra chocolate.'

'You're making very free with my chocolate,' he said. 'There!' I followed his pointing finger. 'Just to the right of that tree.'

'And there's one – look, above the henhouse roof.'

Star by star, the sky came to life.

'Out there,' Sandy said, and I guessed he meant the Western Front, which he'd never mentioned before, 'we used to notice the stars sometimes. It was hard to believe they could keep shining, but they did.' He sighed. 'It's so peaceful here.'

'I know,' I said. 'You couldn't guess, looking out at the hills, that there's still a war on, and the flu! God, Sandy, you should have seen the town today. It was ghostly.' I told him about the closed shops, the suspicious, frightened people, the funeral.

'In France it was like the whole landscape was one hideous festering wound,' he said. 'Maybe now that pus is spreading all over the world, like a new kind of war.'

'Sandy, that's disgusting! And the flu's *not* because of the war, is it? There've been epidemics before.'

He spread his hands. 'What would I know? I'm not a scientist. Here.' He broke the bar of chocolate cream in two and handed me half. I gave it a tentative lick, not quite fancying it now, and went to sit down on my bed.

Sandy stayed leaning against the windowsill, his long legs stretched out. 'About Helen,' he began.

'It's none of my business.' I nibbled round the edge of my chocolate.

But he seemed to want to talk for once. He looked down at the floorboards, his reddish hair hiding his face. I didn't suppose he'd been to a barber while he'd been here. 'Helen's like my baby sister,' he said. 'Our fathers were brothers and we grew up beside each other. I've always sort of protected her.'

'She's not a baby now,' I said. 'She must be the same age as me.'

'She'll be seventeen in January.'

'Well then.'

'But every time she comes she tells me how much my mother misses me, how frail my grandmother is. How they *need* me. If she would just come and *see* me – but she always ends up nagging me to go home.'

'So why don't you?'

He was quiet for a long time, and then said, 'I can't be what they want. They need me to be – you know …'

'Brave and splendid?'

'Hmm.'

I wanted to say he *was* brave, but it would have sounded like I was just trying to make him feel better – and what did I know? But I *did* know a little about Helen. I thought of her eyes darkened with tears. Her loyalty – *he's awfully nice*.

'She said you wouldn't even *see* her.'

'That day. I hadn't slept for – I don't know how long. I was a *mess*.' He pulled at a thread in his jumper. 'I knew if I saw her I'd – oh, you know …' He sounded embarrassed. 'Make a fool of myself. I couldn't stand that.'

'She would understand!' How could anyone be so proud and silly? But I thought of how I'd stopped talking to Helen in the train in case I cried. 'Tell me about her,' I said. 'Not about the visits, or that day – just, about her.'

He gave a brief smile. 'She's clever,' he said. 'She plans to go to Queen's next year to study history. She says she wants to know how the world keeps getting into a mess and how *she* can help it not to.' His voice grew more serious. 'She had another cousin – on her mother's side. Michael. He was killed at Passchendaele. She writes brilliant letters. Well, she *did*.'

More than ever I wanted Helen to come back. For a long, long visit! She sounded exactly the kind of friend I'd always wanted. Maybe she'd even have some ideas about what I could do. I imagined us sharing a flat in Belfast, somewhere airy in a tree-lined street, and we'd have lots of books and radical friends.

'She doesn't sound like the kind of girl you need to protect,' I argued. 'And she seemed strong and determined to me. But she was upset that you wouldn't see her.'

'It would have been worse if I had.' He turned back to the window, arms reaching above his shoulders to grasp the frames.

It was easier to talk to the back of his head. 'You said she *wrote* good letters?'

'She's stopped. I can't blame her.'

'Why don't *you* write? No' – as he shook his head – 'let me finish. You don't have to *see* her. But you could try to explain.' I remembered Mam refusing to write to Rose, saying she'd wait for her to apologise first. Only Rose never did. 'She said' – I frowned, wanting to get this exactly right – 'that she hated giving up on things. But she didn't like making an idiot of herself either. *Flogging a dead horse*, is how she put it. And she cried.' I felt disloyal telling him that but I needed him to understand.

'Helen hardly ever cries.'

I shrugged, realised I'd finished my chocolate, and started to twist the silver paper into a tiny cup. 'That proves how upset she was. Honestly, Sandy, one letter won't kill you.'

'Now *you're* nagging me.'

'Believe me, this is *not* nagging. If I wanted to nag you, you'd know all about it.'

He gave a little laugh. 'I bet I would. You're not one for a quiet life, are you?'

'Not this quiet. I'd like a job or *something*. But now's not the right time – nothing seems permanent – so I'm in a kind of limbo.'

'Nothing's seemed permanent to me since 1914.'

'Have you been in the army all that time?'

He nodded. 'Left school in June, joined up in August. We all thought we were so *lucky* – to be given this chance to prove ourselves. Christ!' He shook his head. 'Half my class is dead now.'

I bit my lip. I thought of Sadie and Lil, and the laughs we had, and everyone in Millside Street School. Tried to imagine half the seats in Miss Braithwaite's class empty. I'd always been jealous of the boys.

'But the war's over for *you* now?' I asked.

'Honourable discharge.' His voice hardened at the word *honourable*, or maybe I imagined it. 'They've had to lower their standards, but half blind, with an arm that's not up to holding a gun, and nerves shot to shreds – they won't lower them that far. I'd be a liability.'

'But you've done your bit! Aren't you glad to be safely out of it?'

He shrugged. 'Being safe when others are still over there – *glad*'s not the right word.'

'Is that why you won't go home?' I dared to ask.

'What do you mean?'

'You push Helen away; you come to live with strangers; you choose a room where nobody can hear you scream – until I did, I mean ...' I rushed on; we'd never talked about that night. 'Are you sure you're not just punishing yourself?'

Before he could answer, Nancy's voice on the landing called, 'Stella?' and the door opened.

'Oh,' she said when she saw Sandy, and her mouth tightened. 'Captain Reid, I'd prefer you *not* to be in Stella's bedroom.'

Sandy's hands slid down the window-frames, and he left the room without a word.

'Nancy!' I said, my face burning. 'We were only *talking*. We were at opposite ends of the room!'

'Shhh.'

'I don't care who hears me! I haven't done anything wrong and neither has Sandy.' I felt as if she had flayed the skin off my face.

'He's a young man. And you're a young girl. In my care. You should know better. I don't mind you being friends but – Stella!' She rubbed at her face. 'I know you've been brought up to be *modern* but even you can't imagine that it's acceptable for you to entertain a man in your room. Your *bedroom*!'

I laughed. *Entertaining a man!* Nancy looked shocked, but if I didn't laugh I might scream. 'Are you saying I'm just like my mother? That I can't be trusted?'

'It's not that.'

'Sandy, then? You don't trust *him*?'

'No, I –'

'Look, Nancy. I don't have a pash on Sandy or anything ridiculous like that,' I said truthfully.

'That's all very well, but he's a man, and you never know –'

'Oh come on! You think he won't be able to help himself? You don't know much about men, do you?'

She bridled at this, playing with the button at her collar. 'I sincerely hope you don't either!'

'I know enough to treat them like normal people! The way you old cats pussyfoot around him is ridiculous! No wonder he hardly comes out of his room. And when he does, you – you treat him like a monster and chase him back in again!' My voice rose shrilly; I was stupidly close to tears of indignation. 'That's the only time he's ever been in my room, and it was only to share some chocolate.' How stupid it sounded. And Sandy, next door, had probably heard every word.

Nancy fiddled with her hair, taking a pin out of her bun and ramming it back in. When she spoke again she sounded worried more than cross. I felt bad about calling her an old cat. 'And *you've* never been in *his* room, I take it? There are *proprieties*, Stella, and they do matter. Even when the world seems upside down. *Especially* then.'

I hesitated. 'No,' I said. 'Course I haven't.'

16

I gloomed in my room, listening to complete silence from next door. What if Sandy didn't *want* to be friends anymore? I wouldn't blame him. And just when I'd made some progress with getting him and Helen together! I bet he'd stop helping with the gardening now too. Probably never come out of his room. Minnie would be back soon, and take his meals again, or Nancy might do it.

But Minnie wasn't coming back. That was one of the shocks at dinner.

'Mrs Mahon died yesterday,' Nancy said. 'Apparently she got up to light the lamp, and just dropped dead. Though the baby's thriving.'

'Och, the poor wee mite,' Mrs Phillips said, and made the soppy face people do about babies. 'Thank God Minnie's of an age to take over.'

'It's a pity it wasn't the other way round,' I said. 'The Mahons don't need another child, especially not now.'

'Stella!' everyone said.

'I'm only being practical. Poor Minnie, stuck with a

baby.' And no mother: I knew what that was like. Now she'd be an unpaid drudge. I might fret at not being allowed to do much, but I knew I wouldn't swap.

I met Sandy's eye to see if he might agree, but he stared at his plate as he had since the moment he had sat down.

That was the other shock. Sandy had come down to dinner, slipping into a seat without a word. He looked unnaturally tidy, wearing a jacket and tie, his hair combed back. He was completely silent, and ate little, and when he reached for the water jug to pour himself a glass, his hand shook and water slopped on the cloth. Nancy had said only, 'How nice that you've joined us, Captain Reid!' and set a place for him. Mrs Phillips and Miss McKay twittered and looked as if they wanted to fuss, but Nancy immediately told us about Minnie's mother, and that distracted attention from him.

Kit had had dinner early, to go on the night shift. I ate my cheese and onion pie, trying to work out why I was so glad she wasn't here for Sandy's first dinner with the household. It was true that I didn't have a pash on Sandy. I'd never had romantic feelings about young men. Maybe I was a late developer. Or else I'd been brought up so much to think about fighting for better lives for women that there wasn't time to bother about boys.

'Will you get a new maid now?' Miss McKay asked. 'Minnie has a sister the right age. I've seen a sturdy wee thing with a toddler on her hip, picking blackberries in the loaning.'

'Sissy,' Nancy said. 'She must be about thirteen. But Minnie will need her.'

'And surely you wouldn't have anyone from that house of pestilence?' Mrs Phillips asked, dabbing her mouth with her napkin.

'Captain Reid, will you be joining us from now on?' Miss McKay asked. She sat with her head perched slightly to the side, like an eager puppy.

Sandy cleared his throat. 'Uh, yes. Given the difficulty with servants I think I should do my bit.'

I saw Mrs Phillips about to rush in with some nonsense about our brave hero having more than done his bit, and I knew Sandy would hate it. He already looked supremely uncomfortable, sweat beading his upper lip, and one hand holding the other to stop it shaking. *Leave him alone!* I wanted to tell everyone. *Let him eat in peace.*

It was up to me to rescue him. 'I got ever so many bulbs in town,' I said. 'It'll be lovely when they come up.' Nobody looked interested. I thought of all the news I'd read today. Perhaps I could tell them that the flu was rampant in Belfast Jail? But I could imagine Mrs Philips saying that prisoners deserved all they got. I needed something more dramatic, so I said, 'I read the most awful story in the *Belfast Telegraph*. A woman in London – a soldier's wife – swallowed three kitchen knives and died.'

'Stella!' Nancy clutched her throat.

I pressed on. 'It said she must have gone mad after the flu. Can you imagine it – swallowing a knife? *Three* knives?'

Mrs Phillips murmured, 'In my day girls were seen and not heard.'

'I'd have hated that,' I said.

Nancy gave me a little smile and said, 'Well, I think we're *mostly* glad that things are different now. Sometimes I wish *I'd* been heard a little bit more.'

'You will be soon,' I said, grateful for the chance to move on to a subject I loved. 'There's going to be an election any day, and you'll be able to vote.'

Her face brightened, and then fell. 'Well, yes,' she said, 'I suppose so. I can't think who I'll vote for, though.'

Mrs Phillips's mouth went cats-bottomish. 'I'd like to hope there would be no question about that. The Sinn Féiners are getting above themselves since their ridiculous rebellion in 1916. It will be up to good unionists like ourselves to keep them out.' She stabbed a carrot as if it were a particularly tough Sinn Féiner.

Brilliant! A political argument! Mentally I rolled up my sleeves. I thought of my heroine, Winifred Carney, in the GPO in 1916. I bet silly Mrs Phillips hadn't even heard of her.

'Ireland *should* be ruled by the Irish,' I said. 'It seems simple to me. A workers' republic!' Hadn't Nancy said Rose had got involved with Republicanism and trade unionism?

'Well!' Mrs Phillips drew herself up and looked at me, eyes popping. 'It might seem simple to you, young lady, but you're English. You can have no idea –'

'I'm as Irish as you are!'

Mrs Phillips spluttered. 'I do *not* consider myself *Irish*,' she said, as if the word conveyed only bogland and pigs in the kitchen. 'This is Ulster. Loyal to the crown.' She drew her cardigan around her.

Miss McKay sighed. 'Politics at dinner? Oh dear.' She made a little joke about this being what happened when men came to table, and I burned with indignation because in fact *I* had started the political conversation.

'Captain Reid.' Mrs Phillips turned to Sandy. 'Having served king and country, I expect *you* wouldn't want to see Ulster sold down the river?'

Sandy speared a piece of pastry with his fork. Then he said, 'I fought side by side with Irish Catholic troops at Messines. They were doing the same as us, only *not* always with the blessing of their communities. So – no, I'm not that bothered about either Home Rule *or* king and country. There are things that matter more.'

'Such as?' Mrs Phillips demanded.

'A proper standard of living. Some of the men in my battalion hadn't seen a decent meal till they got into the army. Fairness.' He paused. 'Peace.' He said the last word the way you might say *Father Christmas* or *unicorns*.

'I didn't think *you'd* have such revolutionary ideas, Captain Reid,' Mrs Phillips said.

'It's not revolutionary!' I cut in. 'It's how things should be.' I felt a stab of loss – this was just the kind of thing Mam talked about all the time.

Nancy started collecting plates. 'There's rice pudding,' she said. 'Stella, would you go and fetch it, please?'

When I came back with the rice pudding the women were talking about knitting, and Sandy was pleating and unpleating his napkin. Such a waste of conversation!

17

When I went outside next morning with a trug full of bulbs Sandy was leaning against a tree, smoking. He stubbed out his cigarette and straightened up when he saw me.

'I did it.' He took a white envelope from his pocket. 'I wrote to Helen. I told her – well, I said sorry I'd been so –'

'Stupid?'

'*Uncommunicative* is the word I used.'

'Good. There's a postbox at the crossroads. If you run down and post it now, it'll get collected at twelve. She'll get it tomorrow.' I imagined Helen getting the letter, being thrilled, sprinting for the next train. That's what *I'd* have done.

He slipped the envelope back into his pocket. 'I'll give you a hand first.' He looked up at the sky. 'It's going to rain.'

Planting bulbs should be lovely. But I soon found the constant stooping back-breaking, especially as we were racing to beat the inky clouds. We worked at opposite ends of the bed, the trug between us, and Sandy was faster than me, and better at digging. This annoyed me so much I redoubled my efforts until my face burned and my back screamed.

'It's not a competition,' Sandy said.

'I don't want to get left behind.'

'Look,' he said. 'I'm bigger than you. And stronger. And more used to physical work.'

I jammed my trowel into the ground, wincing when it struck a root. 'I thought you officers stood back and let the men do all the hard work?'

'Not exactly. I got my hands dirty.'

I sucked at a blister rising on my thumb. 'I want to get them in before the rain. And Mrs Phillips said November was too late for bulbs and they'll come to nothing.'

'Don't listen to her. This bed will look great in the spring.'

'D'you think you'll still be here to see it?' I asked.

He frowned. 'I'm not planning on going anywhere. Unless I get struck down by the *foul pestilence*.'

He imitated Mrs Phillips's nasal whine, and I giggled and then said, 'Don't joke.'

He joggled in the earth to make the hole bigger then dropped a bulb in. 'I'm sorry. It's just – up here' – he gestured round the garden – ' everything seems so far away. Politics – family – war –'

'But it's not. Minnie's house is – what – half a mile away?' I shuddered. 'As for *politics*' – I grinned at the memory of the heated discussion at dinner – 'that's never far away. It affects everything. Every bit of people's lives.'

'Ye-es.' Sandy sounded unsure. He scrabbled in his pocket for his cigarettes, but didn't light up immediately. 'I was brought up to believe in the union – you know, Ireland staying part of Britain. My father signed the Ulster Covenant. When the chance came to fight for king and country I didn't hesitate. It's what my father would have wanted. It's what all my friends did. Our *duty*.' He tapped his cigarette and lit a match from a rather squashed box.

'So – do you still want Ulster to stay in the union?'

'Yes. But if – well, *when* there's Home Rule, Ireland will be partitioned – Ulster will never accept Dublin rule. And that seems to go against what we've been fighting for. I'd like countries to come together more – not split up into tiny suspicious states looking over their shoulders at each other. When the war ends things will have to be sorted out over here, and I don't know how it can happen without more fighting. And it's not just about Home Rule now. Sinn Féin want complete independence.' He shivered. 'I can't bear the thought of more bloodshed.'

'But some things are worth fighting for. If women hadn't *fought* for the vote, they wouldn't have got it.'

'Most people say they got it because the suffragettes gave up their militancy to join the war effort.'

I snorted. 'Rubbish! People say that because they don't want to admit the suffragettes won!'

'The vote was won in Parliament.'

'It wouldn't have been without the suffragettes! *They* changed people's minds. They fought and starved and *died* to make women's lives better.'

'Oh, come on, Stella. Burning buildings, throwing bricks, blowing up post-boxes – not exactly noble tactics. And didn't the Pankhursts shove off to France out of the way?'

'And how noble were *your* tactics when you were killing people in France?'

Sandy's good eye widened in shock.

'I'm sorry – I don't mean *you*, personally. I mean – in war, things – people – get hurt. The suffragettes only damaged property. Not people. And *Sylvia* Pankhurst didn't shove off anywhere. She's organising women in the East End of London. She never gave up the struggle. *And* she's against the war.' I dug hard into the soil.

'There's no need to get so het up,' Sandy said. 'The vote *has* been won. And they announced last week that women can even stand for election, so now *you* can get into Parliament and change the world.'

I gave him a sideways glance. 'Maybe I will.'

'You sound like Helen. Well, you mightn't make more of a mess of it than men have done.'

The mention of Helen reminded me. 'Your letter! If you don't dash to the postbox now you'll miss the collection.'

Sandy placed another bulb into the ground. 'Better finish this off. I might go this afternoon.' He looked down the garden to the loaning, and somehow I knew he didn't want to go as far as to the crossroads. It wasn't laziness; he had worked harder than I had, his cheeks red with the effort of digging and a film of sweat on his face despite the cold air. It was some kind of fear. Like me and the motorcar, maybe.

'Will I go with you?' I offered. 'It's not far.'

He shook his head. 'Don't nag.'

I opened my mouth to tell him not to be silly, it wasn't nagging, and what was the point of going to all the bother of *finally* writing a letter and then not taking a mere ten-minute stroll to the postbox – and then I closed it. He was right. It could wait. I wanted Helen to come and stay so much that my motives for encouraging him were probably a bit confused.

'Sorry,' I said instead. 'None of my business.'

'Were you head girl at school?' Sandy asked with a slight grin.

'It wasn't that kind of school. But if there'd been a head girl, it might have been me.'

And then I was very good and talked about nothing more contentious than bulbs for the rest of the morning.

After lunch it rained in hard icy sheets and even I was glad to stay indoors and read by the drawing-room fire. Nancy was baking Christmas cakes and the warm spicy smell filled the house. I finished *Mansfield Park*, which I hadn't liked as much as the others, and ran upstairs to get *Northanger Abbey*. A damp draft gusted into my room and I dashed over to shut the window.

And saw Sandy, in his dark overcoat and cap, standing at the gate. He looked down the loaning and reached out his hand to the gate. He opened it but didn't go through.

He just stood. I watched, knowing he couldn't see me, but hardly wanting to breathe. After a while he pulled the gate closed again, and turned back and walked towards the house, head down, shoulders stooped.

I knew it wasn't the rain that had stopped him.

18

After breakfast next day I followed Sandy upstairs. Nancy, crossing the hall with a tray, frowned but what could she do? I was only going to my room.

'Do you want *me* to take the letter?' I offered, at the turn of the stairs outside the bathroom.

'What do you mean?'

I chose my words carefully. 'If you don't feel up to the walk?'

'I'm fine.'

'Of course.' I wasn't going to tell him I had seen his struggle yesterday. 'But – well, if you're busy – or anything – I could.'

'You know I'm not busy.'

'It would be no bother.' I tried to hide how much I wanted him to give me the letter. Of course it would be better for *him* to go himself. But the most important thing was Helen getting his apology. It didn't matter who posted it.

'I should …' His voice died away. 'Oh, all right.'

'I'll run down at once,' I said, before he could change his mind.

Only I didn't run. I did something better. Leaning against the railings of the front garden was Kit's bicycle. She must have been too tired after the night shift to wheel it round to the shed. I could do it as a kind gesture. No sense in leaving a good bicycle outdoors to rust.

I placed my hands on the black rubberised handlebars and looked at its big glistening wheels. Kit wouldn't want it until evening. On a bicycle I could be at the postbox in less than five minutes. Downhill all the way. It would be fun. And the post was collected at ten on Saturdays, and it was nearly that now, so cycling would mean I caught it, and Sandy's letter wouldn't have to languish in the box all weekend, doing no good to anyone. It could start its journey to Belfast and spare Helen an extra day of worrying about her cousin. Kit should be proud to lend a bike for such a noble cause.

I flung my leg over the low bar, bunched up my skirt so it wouldn't get caught, and rattled out of the yard. At first I wobbled, but once I hit the loaning I got into my rhythm and by the time I reached the road, the bicycle was spinning along sweetly under me. The handlebars felt solid, and the wind rushed at my face. I wanted people to see me, to wonder who this modern, adventurous girl was, but there wasn't a soul around.

Five minutes later I pushed the envelope into the postbox's slot with a sense of its importance. *Helen Reid, 22 Cyclamen Terrace, Belfast 6.* She would read it tomorrow

– no, tomorrow was Sunday. Monday, then. She might get straight onto a train and come down and see him! If her school were closed – many were – she might even be able to stay for a few days. Of course she would want to see Sandy mainly, but the three of us might do things together. She would have to share my room – she could have my bed and I'd make do with a shakedown. I wouldn't mind a bit.

I hesitated at the crossroads, the bicycle like a trusty steed. I didn't want to go home. I wanted adventure. If I went right down the hill I would be in Cuanbeg. But I had no money and I didn't fancy glooming around watching funeral processions in the cutting sea wind. I turned the bicycle left, up towards the hills. I would go and see if I could find out what had happened to Rose.

19

So many times I nearly turned back. The streets of Manchester had not prepared me for the steep drag up the foothills of the mountains. Despite the cold November air I was soon sweltering inside my clothes, legs shrieking with effort. But I'm not a turning-back kind of girl, and goodness knows when I'd next have the chance. Kit might never lend her bicycle again, especially as I hadn't asked permission, and it wasn't certain that Nancy would buy me one for Christmas. And though it was hard work, at least it wasn't terrifying, like the motorcar. Or nauseating.

I lost my way a few times, but eventually I found the farm Nancy had pointed out, and I was glad enough to stop and wheel my bike up the rutted lane. Trees overhung it on each side, making it dark and scary – at least, some girls might have been scared. Chickens scratched around, scraggy and noisy, and a cow leaned over the wall and mooed so loudly that I nearly fell over the bicycle, which was fast becoming splashed with mud, as were my shoes and skirt.

The house came into view, a small farmhouse, shabby but not as unkempt as the Mahons'. My wheels sounded loud on the rough yard, but the door remained shut. I knocked and waited for a long time. Anxiety fluttered in my chest. This was stupid. I didn't know Rose's parents. They'd been against her activities – *mortified*, Nancy had said, especially when she started getting arrested. They might not know where she was now, and chances were – I had to face this – she was dead. The last time I'd seen her, she'd been recovering from her worst hunger strike, and had looked terrible, all bruised and skinny, her throat so torn from the force-feeding tube that she could hardly speak.

Something rattled above me. A window was pushed open and a woman's voice called: 'Who is it?' I tilted my head back but I couldn't see her face.

'Um. I was hoping to find out about Rose Sullivan. I'm Peggy Graham's daughter.' I said it without hope.

'*What?*' The window opened wider and this time she put her head and shoulders out. '*Stella?*' Her lips pushed out into a wide smile. 'Stay there!' she said. 'Don't move one inch!' Her face disappeared from the window and I heard her talk to someone in the room, presumably telling them about this unexpected visitor.

I heard stairs clatter and then the door pulled open with a squeak and Rose herself stood in front of me.

20

Rose! Her hair wasn't as bright, but her dark eyes flashed just like I remembered, and the wide smile was the same too. She was still thin, though fatter than when she'd got out of prison, but her tweed skirt was pulled out of shape by a pregnant belly. She grabbed my hands.

'Are you here on holiday?' she asked. Her voice was hoarse, as if her throat had never quite recovered from the force-feeding tube. 'Where's Peggy?'

'Oh,' I said. 'She died.'

'No!' Rose's eyes filled with instant tears, and I remembered how she had always shown her feelings. 'How?'

'Flu.'

Rose clapped her hand to her mouth. 'Oh, God! I should never have lost touch!'

I tried to say something but I couldn't.

Rose looked me up and down. 'And look at you, all grown up. But come away in.' She stepped aside and pulled the door wide and I followed her straight into a low, dim kitchen with a smoking turf fire. Bread cooled on a rough table. 'I was baking,' she said. She set a kettle over the fire and raked the coals. 'You'll take tea?'

I nodded.

'How did you find me?'

'Determination and ingenuity,' I said, because it was too boring to tell the truth.

She laughed, sniffed and wiped her eyes with her sleeve. Even though my feelings about Mam were uncomfortably close to the surface, something inside me relaxed for the first time since I had taken the Liverpool boat. Rose's kitchen wasn't very comfy, with only a high-backed wooden settle to sit on, but it was warm in front of the big stone hearth. Rose spooned tea into a brown teapot and set out three cups. It was funny to see her so domesticated.

'I'll call Charlie,' she said. She went to the stairs that led out of the kitchen and called, 'Charlie, will you take a drop of tea?'

From upstairs a man's voice called something I didn't catch. And then a rattle of coughing made me flinch. 'It's not flu, is it?' I asked.

Rose shook her head. 'Do you think I'd have let you in if it were? No – we both had it last month. But Charlie was gassed in France. He's grand for days and then, when he overdoes it, he's like this. And he can't *not* overdo it, because there's nobody else. I do what I can but now I'm expecting I have to take it easier.' She placed her hands over her belly.

'I never thought I'd end up back here,' she went on. 'But Daddy died and Mammy went away to her sister in Dublin. And with Joe long dead – well, I sort of ended up with the farm. We're trying to make a go of it, and at least it's a roof over our heads, but I never saw myself as a farmer's wife. And Charlie's from the Falls Road in Belfast. He didn't know one end of a cow from another six months ago.'

On the high mantelshelf above the fire, something familiar glittered: a suffragette hunger-strike medal. She saw me looking, and shuddered. 'I still have nightmares,' she said.

'I remember you being with us just after this.'

'I wish I hadn't fallen out with Peggy,' she said. 'A million times I thought I should write, but – I waited for her. And then – well, other things got in the way.'

'What things?'

'I came back to Ireland. Got involved in Republicanism. It was an exciting time. Fighting for a free Ireland – not just the vote for women.' Her eyes were wistful as if she missed all that excitement.

The stairs creaked and a man came into the room. Like Rose, he looked older than he probably was, with grey in his brown hair. His hair and shirt were rumpled, as if he'd been lying down. And though I knew I'd never met him before, something about him was familiar.

'You're welcome here,' he said to me. He had a different accent from the people round here. Harsher. 'I'm away out to the yard, Rose,' he said. 'Need to patch that roof.' He leaned on the mantelshelf and hacked out a barrage of coughs.

She handed him a cup. 'You'll go nowhere without a cup of tea inside you.'

He sat on the settle, shifting as if in pain, flexing his leg, and drank the tea quickly, but shook his head when Rose offered to cut a slice of fresh bread. He placed his cup on the table and got up, and for the first time I noticed that he walked with a distinct limp. He took a tweed cap from a hook on the door, nodded to us, and shuffled out. Rose saw me watching.

'He lost a leg at Messines,' she said. 'He has a wooden one but it pains him sometimes.' She set her own cup down. 'But sure, many's a one never came back. I'm lucky.'

'But you – you were so against the war! When Mam went into munitions you called her a traitor and –'

'I know.' Rose sounded weary. 'And I specially didn't believe Irishmen should get involved. Let the English sort it out, I've always thought. It did come between us. We nearly didn't get married at all. But – well, I loved him too much for that. And I'd already lost Peggy. Maybe that taught me something.' She frowned. 'We met at work. He was the shop steward for the men, me for the women. His family were against us getting married. An activist and jailbird!' She stood up, pressing her hand into the small of her back. 'I'm not due till March,' she said. 'I don't know why I'm so big. There's twins in Charlie's family. I hope it's not, though I suppose we'd cope. Sure what else is there?'

She talked to me like I was an adult. Like Mam had done.

'Can I help?' I asked.

'I don't suppose you know how to milk a cow? Or muck out a byre?'

I shook my head, disappointed at such dull things. 'I can do shorthand and typing, and I've become quite good at gardening,' I offered. 'But I've hardly ever seen a cow.'

'Shorthand and typing?'

'I went to commercial college in Manchester. Mam hoped I'd get an office job and not have to go into a mill or a factory. I can't imagine myself in an office, though. Unless I could be like Winifred Carney – she's my heroine.'

'Winnie!' Rose said. 'I knew her quite well in Belfast.'

'Really? Oh my!'

'We went to a lot of the same meetings. Some of the people in the Republican cause weren't happy when I married Charlie – him having fought for the King – but Winnie stood by me. She said the cause of labour was bigger than that. Och – but I'm sure you won't want to hear all this political talk.'

I laughed. 'Yes, I do! I've been having withdrawal symptoms at Nancy's. This feels like …' I didn't want to say like coming home; it sounded too soppy. 'It's a bit boring at Nancy's,' I said instead.

'I'm sure there's plenty for you to do in that big house.'

'I'd rather help *you*.'

'It's a fair distance,' she said. 'But I see you have the bike.'

'It's not mine,' I admitted. The clock on the high

mantelshelf wheezed and chimed – twelve times. 'Oh lordy!' I said. 'I ought to go. But I'll come back, I promise. If I don't, it's only because I can't get the bike.'

In the yard Charlie was pushing a wheelbarrow full of wet cowdung. It listed and nearly toppled – I wasn't sure if it was because of his leg, or because the barrow itself was so old. He lifted his cap and drew a grimed hand across his forehead. 'You're welcome here any time,' he said. 'It gave Rose a quare lift to see you. She talked a lot about your mammy. She was very sorry when they fell out. Especially when they'd been through so much together. Her standing by your mammy when your da –' He broke off.

Unexpected tears pricked my eyes. I looked away, and into the far distance, where the mountains were in silhouette against a milky sky.

'Sometimes I can't get used to the quiet here,' Charlie said. 'The peace. We don't even get into town these days since our old horse has been lame.' He sighed.

I knew now who he reminded me of. And the best idea I'd ever had dropped into my head. 'I know somebody who might help you on the farm,' I said.

'We can't afford help.'

'He wouldn't need paying. He needs something to do. He's been blinded in one eye but he's a good worker. He's been helping me in the garden. I'll ask him as soon as I get home.'

I imagined Sandy and me coming out here; the satisfaction of hard work and helping people. Sandy and Charlie would become friends – they had so much in common – while Rose told me more about Mam, all the things Nancy wouldn't or couldn't tell me. And Sandy would grow happy and sleep at night and Helen would come and visit and be so grateful to me. Really, I was excellent at fixing people's lives. My heart skipped.

'Soldier, was he?'

'Yes, a captain.'

Charlie gave a mirthless laugh and started to push the barrow again. 'I don't see a captain wanting to shovel shite for a private.'

I tilted my chin. 'I wouldn't have thought Rose Sullivan's husband would have been so reactionary,' I said. 'Just you wait. I'll sort it out.'

And I freewheeled most of the way home, the wind blowing my hair and my heart singing.

21

'Where on earth have you been with my bike?'

As I dismounted outside Cliffside House, my heart stopped singing. Kit stood with her hands on her hips, her face dark red. She must have been lying in wait.

Nancy materialised behind her. 'Thank God! I thought you were dead in a ditch.'

'I …'

Mrs Phillips appeared, holding her wrap around her as if she was braving the cold air especially on my behalf. 'So thoughtless – your poor aunt was beside herself.'

Kit leapt down the steps and grabbed at her bicycle. 'It's filthy!'

'I was going to clean it.' I should have gone straight round to the back and hosed it down before anyone saw me. But I'd been so elated by finding Rose and my wonderful idea, and –

I looked at them all and realised that I couldn't say any of that. I tried to look contrite – well, I *was* sorry about worrying Nancy, and I didn't blame Kit for being cross about the bike.

'She's very flushed,' Mrs Phillips said. 'I shouldn't wonder if she's sickening for something. So irresponsible – going goodness knows where and picking up goodness knows what, and bringing it back here.' She held her scarf to her mouth. How often, I wondered, was someone tempted to strangle her with that scarf?

But I suppressed that unsisterly thought, and said, 'I lost track of time. I only went for a ride. I'm sorry for not asking you, Kit. But you were asleep.' Before she could say anything I rushed on, 'I'm going to clean the bike this instant. It'll be shining.'

'It had better be.'

I looked at Nancy. She was very pale. 'I'm sorry I worried you. But I'm not a child. I can look after myself.'

'Going off for hours without a word seems childish to me,' she said, her voice tight.

'Even poor Captain Reid was out looking for you. Far and wide!' Mrs Phillips said, turning to go back inside with an exaggerated shiver.

Really? I remembered Sandy standing at the gate yesterday, clearly unable to make himself go through it. If he'd been looking for me *far and wide*, maybe he'd got over his – whatever it was. And that could only be a good thing. It looked like my unplanned trip had been of benefit all round. I couldn't wait to find Sandy and tell him my plans.

I didn't have to wait long. When I wheeled the bicycle round to the yard, he was leaning against the wall behind the shed, smoking. I grinned at him, zinging with triumph.

'So,' he said. 'You aren't dead in the ditch or taken by white slave traders or run off to join the circus?'

'Which did you think was most likely?'

'Circus.' He flicked his ash.

'Thank you for looking for me.'

A muscle jumped in his jaw.

'It must have taken a lot for you to go – *far and wide*, Mrs Phillips said.' I gave a light laugh. '*I've* never known you to leave the garden.'

'Don't mention it.' The tone didn't mean *you're welcome*. It meant *shut up*. So I did.

'Will you help me clean the bicycle?' I fetched some cloths and a bucket which I filled from the pump.

'Did you post the letter?'

I handed him a sponge. 'Of course. But – oh, Sandy, wait till you hear where I've been!' I started to tell him about the farm, and Charlie, and Rose being pregnant – his eyes flickered in embarrassment at the word and I said, 'Oh come on, Sandy – it's almost 1919! Did you expect me to say she was in an *interesting condition*?' I pulled a clump of leaves from the spokes of the back wheel. 'But, Sandy – the *best* thing – I said we'd help them.'

'*We?*'

'You and me. Even *I* admit Charlie needs a man's help. And *you* need something to do. It's not that far. You could take me a backie on the bike. Or if we can't borrow it' – I spun the wheel to get more of the dried mud off and Sandy jerked back out of the way. 'Sorry!' I said. 'If we can't take the bike maybe Nancy would lend you the car. You can drive, can't you?' I quaked at the memory of being in a car, but I didn't want to admit any problems so I rushed on. 'Which would be *exceptionally* noble of me, because the only other time I was in a car I was sick as a dog' – I grimaced – 'but it might be different with *you* driving. *Not* that I think men are better drivers than women, but –'

'Whoa!' Sandy held up his hand. 'I don't even know these people.'

'But Charlie's just like you – I mean, *he's* suffered in the war.' And surely it was worse to lose a leg than the sight of one eye? 'I thought you could – you know, talk about it, maybe …' My voice trailed off.

Sandy was staring at me. 'Why would I do that?'

'Well, then, *not* talk about it. Just – sort of help each other.'

He shook his head. 'Stella – you can't go round organising people's lives! And I don't know the first thing about farming.'

'He only needs a bit of brawn.'

'And Nancy *wouldn't* lend us the car, not for a jaunt like that. She wouldn't let me take you out without a chaperone.'

I stamped my foot and water sloshed over the edge of the bucket. 'Don't be so old-fashioned! And *ungrateful*! I'm trying to *help* people.' I sounded a bit of a prig, even to myself.

'People don't always want help.'

'You wanted me to post your letter.'

'*You* wanted to.'

I clamped my mouth shut and wrung out my cloth. 'Well, anyway,' I muttered, 'I'll help them myself if it comes to it. Even if I have to walk every step.'

'Which you probably will,' Sandy said. 'I don't see anyone lending you another bicycle in a hurry.' He gestured with one foot to a deep scrape on the rear mudguard which I was sure hadn't been there before I set off.

'Blast! That must have been from when I skidded to avoid a hen. She'll kill me.'

'You could hide it. If you rub it down with some very fine sandpaper and then build it up again with enamel paint. There's some in the shed. If you know what you're doing it'll look as good as new.'

'I *don't* know what I'm doing.'

'Pity.' He lit another cigarette.

'Do *you*?'

'Oh, yes. Easy.'

'So would you help me – at least, show me what to do?'

He sighed. 'You're the *most* aggravating girl.'

'I know. But if you help me, I promise not to aggravate for the rest of the day.'

'What about tomorrow?'

I spread my hands in a hopeless gesture. 'I can't make any promises about tomorrow.' But I grinned. I didn't want a quarrel. Already that letter was on its way to Helen and I wanted to make sure that when she came to visit, as she surely would, Sandy'd let me be part of things. So I rubbed meekly at the scratch with the sandpaper he found for me in the shed. And let him boss me. All in a good cause.

And as I sat back and held out the tin of black enamel, while Sandy painted over the newly rubbed-down area with a hand that was steadier than I had seen it, I let myself imagine that same hand gripping a pitchfork or clapped around Charlie's stooping shoulders as the two men strode side by side to do – my imagination stalled – some farmerish thing. It was summer, and the war was over and Rose and I – and Helen – stood and watched them go, and then turned to each other with smiles of satisfaction. Rose's daughter bounced on her knee and laughed while we fantasised about the new world she would grow up in, as an independent young woman in a free Ireland – because, of course, independence had been won without bloodshed and everyone was happy. Helen and I were best friends, the kind of friends I had always dreamed of, the kind of friends Sadie and Lil had never come close to being. I sighed happily.

'Stella! You're spilling paint all over the cobbles!'

I righted the tin. 'Sorry,' I said. My lips stretched into a huge smile. It would happen. I would make sure it did.

22

It was Kit who brought the news. I heard her shouting even before the whirr of her wheels on the gravel. I looked out of the drawing-room window, where I'd been reading *Northanger Abbey*, and saw her wave a newspaper, standing on her pedals. I flung open the window, ignoring Mrs Phillips's protest about the bitter air.

'It's over!' Kit shouted. 'Germany surrendered! The Armistice has been signed!'

Even though we'd all known this was coming, it seemed unbelievable that it had actually happened. My insides fluttered. 'The war's over!' I shouted to Mrs Phillips, and to my surprise she turned away with a sob, her scarf pressed to her mouth. I ran out of the room and shouted, 'Nancy! Miss McKay! Sandy! The war's over!'

Doors opened. Kit dashed in waving the *Belfast Telegraph*. All the women of the household congregated in the hall and there was hugging and tears and everyone was very kind to Mrs Phillips, and Nancy said how lovely for Miss McKay not to have to worry about the twins any more.

'I'm going to open Daddy's champagne!' she said.

'I hope I'm allowed some,' I said, and everyone laughed. We were all acting a bit, and my role was the *ingénue*. Enthusiastic and a little silly.

'I'll tell Sandy.' I started towards the stairs. Nancy didn't try to stop me. I thundered upstairs, two at a time, and battered on his door.

'Sandy! The war's over!' From inside the bed creaked, I heard the soft thud of a book falling to the floor and the gasp of a caught breath. 'Sandy?' I knocked again. 'Please come out. Nancy's opening champagne.'

Footsteps. He stood in the doorway. 'Over?' he said.

I nodded. 'Will you come down? You, of all people, should celebrate with us.'

'Celebrate?' He wrinkled his forehead.

I let out a long breath. 'I know,' I said. 'There are all the men who won't come back. Your friends. I know. And they do too – Kit will still be nursing. Mrs Phillips's husband will still be dead. It's not just you. Please come down. They need you. You're their – sort of – connection with it.'

A flicker of doubt crossed his face and then he said, 'Of course.'

And he came down with me to the drawing room and shook hands with everyone and accepted a glass of champagne. I took a gulp of mine – delicious, sneeze-making stuff.

'Stella, wait,' Nancy said. 'We must have a toast. Captain Reid – will you do the honours?'

Sandy closed his eyes for a second. I would have loved to make the toast: I could think of a hundred things to say. He looked at the floor. I wondered if he was thinking that he should be playing the role of returning hero with his own people, not us. Helen should have got the letter this morning – what wonderful timing: the war ending and Sandy's apology, all in one day!

'Sandy?' I nudged him.

He cleared his throat. 'I don't know what to say,' he admitted. 'Except – thank God it's over. And – well, here's to peace.'

He raised his glass and everyone chorused, 'Peace!'

Another round of hugs, and everyone laugh-sobbing and shouting so that nobody could have heard a bicycle on the gravel, and even when the front doorbell rang, it had to ring a second time.

'I'll go!' Maybe it was a neighbour come to share the joy.

But it was the telegraph boy. He held out the little brownish rectangle. 'Telegram for Reid.'

I took it eagerly. 'Thank you,' I said. It must be Helen – wiring to say she was on her way. Just as I had done. What a day for miracles!

'Sandy!' He stood in the hall, glass still in one hand, cigarette in the other, hair falling over his face. Perhaps now, I thought, he will go to the barber's. He won't want to look untidy for Helen. But there may not be time, and really, she won't mind. His mother might; for the first time I thought of the possibility that his mother might come too. I shoved the telegram at him, and held out my hands for his cigarette and glass, so he would be free to open it. I had one of those moments of seeing myself from the outside, and very sophisticated I looked, with my champagne glass and cigarette. Though the cigarette was almost smoked down to its tip; he would need to take it back soon if it wasn't going to burn me. Still, it didn't take long to read a telegram.

Sandy's eyes scanned the single sheet. Funny, I thought, how his bad eye moves in unison with the good one even though he can't see out of it.

'When's she coming?' I asked.

He looked up and didn't speak for ages, his mouth working as if it had forgotten what to do. 'She isn't.'

Disappointment plunged through me. 'Oh! Why not?'

Sandy tossed the telegram down on the hall table. 'She's dead.'

He moved towards the stairs, and then, with a long shivering breath, swung round and blundered out the front door, while I stood looking after him, the cigarette burning through my skin.

23

I read it again. Just in case it might magically say something different. But it still read:

> HELEN DIED THIS MORNING. FLU WITH COMPLICATIONS. VERY QUICK. FUNERAL WEDNESDAY. WRITING. MOTHER.

I dashed out after Sandy. The telegraph boy's tracks were fresh on the gravel, thicker treads than Kit's wheels. The telegram's words whirled round my head like a snowstorm: FLU WITH COMPLICATIONS. VERY QUICK. Like Mam. She had gone to bed out of sorts on the Thursday night, tired after a heavy day at the factory and a bad-tempered union meeting. She shouldn't have been in work but she'd already missed some days to nurse me when I'd had it the week before. She woke sweating and coughing and raving with fever, and on Saturday she was dead. I thought of Helen's clear, pale face; the neat features, the tidy shining plait. Tried not to imagine her blue and gasping and frothing at the mouth. I gave a little sob, and I didn't know if it was for Helen or Mam or Sandy or me or just the horribleness of it all. It wasn't ten minutes since we'd been drinking champagne and laughing.

Sandy stopped at the garden gate, exactly where he had been the day he had tried to take the letter. I looked at his straight back, rain darkening his flannel shirt. I hadn't noticed it was raining. He placed his hand on the gate, just like before, and a shudder ran through him. He pulled the gate towards him, very slowly. I don't think he knew I was there but I was so close I could hear every breath. He walked through the gate and down the loaning. I stood in the gateway and looked at his departing back.

'Sandy!' I called. He didn't stop or turn round or slow down. I knew I could say or do nothing to comfort him. I stayed until the cold rain penetrating my jumper made me shiver, and then I went inside to tell Nancy.

24

I was washing the dinner dishes in the scullery when I heard the back door click and Sandy came in, blinking in the light.

'Oh,' he said, when he saw me with the cloth in my hand. I supposed he'd wanted to slip in without seeing anyone. I followed him into the kitchen. His shoes made speckled wet prints on the tiles.

'You're soaked,' I said. 'You should take those wet things off or you'll –'

'Catch my death?'

'We kept you some dinner.'

He shook his head.

'Whiskey?' I suggested. 'I know where she keeps it.'

'Yes.'

I took a clean towel down from the clothes airer over the range and threw it at him. 'You could take the rough off with that.'

He caught the towel but then stood staring at it as if he didn't know how to use it, rain dripping down his face. I recognised the dumb stupor that I'd been in when Mam died. But I'd had things to do to haul me out of my shock – the undertaker to see, people to deal with. Sandy had nothing but the loss. I stepped up beside him and started to rub his hair with the towel. He smelt of smoke and outdoors. After a few seconds he took it from me and finished the job. I fetched him a large glass of whiskey. He downed it like medicine, his teeth chattering on the glass.

'Have a hot bath,' I said, taking it from him.

'Not my night.'

'It's mine. But I'm quite clean.'

Nancy appeared, her face all concern.

'Sandy,' she said. 'I'm so sorry.' And she shook his hand which I remembered people doing when Mam died, even people I didn't know like the undertaker. 'What a cruel blow! Today of all days.'

Sandy nodded.

'Will you travel home tomorrow?' she asked.

'The funeral's Wednesday.'

'If you'd like to borrow the car,' she said. 'It's a long drive, I know – but you might prefer it to the train. More private.'

'It's ages since I've driven.' He looked panicky. 'I don't think I should risk it.'

'The train, then.'

'I could go with you,' I offered.

Nancy shook her head. 'I have plans for you here, Stella.' She chivvied me back out to the scullery on the pretext of washing the whiskey glass.

When we were in there she said, 'You mustn't *crowd* Captain Reid. And a funeral is no place for a little girl.' She made me feel about six. 'It's not like you *knew* Helen. You mustn't intrude on his grief. Now, Miss McKay needs you to wind wool in the drawing room.'

By the time I escaped upstairs I could see, from the sliver of light under his door, that Sandy was in his room. I wanted to ask if he was all right; I wanted to be able to use the proper words like *condolence* and *tragedy* but I knew I'd say the wrong thing. Or cry. And his door looked so unwelcoming.

So I went to bed and lay awake for hours, trying not to think about Helen lying in her coffin at the undertakers' – or at home? I imagined her hair loose round her face, arranged perhaps to hide the horrible blue stain of cyanosis. Or would that disappear after death? I hadn't looked at Mam's face afterwards. The doctor had said I should. 'It comforts people, reassures them the deceased is really dead,' he had said, and I had screamed at him that I *knew* she was dead; nobody who had seen her die in agony could have had the slightest doubt, but then *he* hadn't been there, had he? I had cried and shouted and the doctor had given me something to calm me down and for the next few days I had waded through life half-dopey.

I had not been brave or splendid.

25

'It's for a good cause,' I said. 'War work, really.'

Kit did not say that the war had been over for two days. After all, she was still nursing. The newspaper was full of advice on *What to do when the boys come home* but none of them had actually *come* home yet. Apart from a sense of relief in the pit of everyone's stomach – at least it was in the pit of mine and I assumed other people felt the same – nothing had changed.

'Please?' I said. 'Rose is in the family way, and her husband lost his leg in France, and there's nobody to help, and I promised – but it's too far to walk.'

'Oh, all right,' Kit said. 'I suppose I can walk to Sunny View for once.'

'You're a brick,' I said, which is what the girls in books always said, and sped off to get the bike before she changed her mind.

I stuffed some things in the basket that I thought Rose would like – Monday's *Belfast Telegraph*, with the Armistice announcement; a jar of Nancy's bramble jelly; some yellow wool sent by Miss McKay, and a bunch of lanky rust chrysanthemums from the garden.

The road seemed shorter now I knew where I was going. I overtook Sandy just before the crossroads, trudging along, head down, remote in a dark overcoat. He'd miss the train if he didn't get a move on. Nancy should have let me go with him. For a moment I thought of changing my plans – I could leave the bike at the station; and even if Sandy decided to stay with his family, it wasn't like I'd never got the train from Belfast before, and Rose wasn't actually expecting me *today*. But the way Sandy glanced at me and then back at the road ahead – something about the set of his shoulders – told me he didn't want company. So there was nothing to do but carry on up to the farm, where Rose was glad to see me, though Charlie only gave a quick wave and carried on up the yard, shoulders bowed under the weight of a bale of hay.

I cleaned out the hen-house; washed the kitchen floor; black-leaded the range; ironed five rather threadbare shirts and a voluminous skirt. I felt very virtuous, especially as Rose sat on the settle mending and telling me what a great help I was and how proud Peggy would be of me. *She* didn't think I was *aggravating* and *interfering* and *intrusive*. Rose chatted easily, filling in the years since I'd seen her, asking about Mam and our lives in Manchester.

'I hated being estranged from Peggy,' she said. 'We'd been like sisters. But at the time, it seemed to matter so much – being on opposite sides about the war. I wish I'd written. But I'm not very good at backing down.'

'Neither was she.'

Rose glanced up at the clock above the mantelshelf, and then stood up, laid down her mending, filled the kettle and set it on the range.

'Would you call Charlie?' she asked. 'If I don't make him stop he'll work all day and half the night. He's been like that since he got back. Restless. Like he doesn't want to stop and remember. I don't know what to say to him half the time.'

'I'm restless too,' I said. 'I mean – I always like to be *doing* things. But it's just how I am – I'm not trying to forget anything.'

Rose spooned tea into the pot and said nothing.

Charlie sniffed when he saw the *Belfast Telegraph*.

'Unionist propaganda,' he said. 'I won't have it in the house. *Irish News*, that's the paper.'

Rose looked mortified. 'Charlie! It was very kind of Ste–'

I tilted my chin. I didn't need anyone to fight my battles for me. 'I'm sorry you feel that way. But it's the only paper Nancy *will* have in the house, so it's that or nothing. If you think I've the time or the money to cycle into town and buy you the *Irish News* you can damn well do it yourself. Use it to light the fire if you like. I won't offend you with it again.'

Charlie gave me a very straight look and then laughed, and said well, he supposed news was news, and Rose gave me a scone fresh from the oven.

'Good for you,' she said after he had limped out again.

'I'm always making allowances because he's had such a bad time. But maybe that's not what he needs.'

What he needed, I thought, was practical help on the farm. I'd have to make it happen! It mightn't be the great society-changing gesture I longed for, but it would be something. And it would help Sandy too.

Cycling home in the near-dusk, I wondered what it would be like when all the soldiers finally came home. Millions of men walking round with horrible memories. Millions of women making allowances.

And then, slowing down for the crossroads before the loaning, thinking that I really had earned my dinner and hoping it would be something nice, I saw a figure standing there. A tall black shadow against the purpling sky. My heart hammered, until I realised it was Sandy, more or less where I had last seen him. My first thought was, *Hooray! He came back!*

But the closer I got the less horayish I felt. There was something weird about the way he stood. Still. Looking at nothing. Something I hadn't known I knew scratched at my mind: that in the past, suicides were buried at crossroads. I shivered and pedalled faster, willing the black shadow to move, to live, to turn back into the real, breathing Sandy.

'Sandy?' My voice was hesitant. He mustn't have heard; not a muscle moved. I called louder. 'Sandy!' And then scrambled off the bike and shouted, running the last few yards.

He still didn't move. I was right beside him now. 'What are you doing? How could you get back so soon?'

He didn't react. I placed my hand on his arm. Even through the wool of his coat sleeve his arm was as rigid and cold as a statue.

'Sandy? Are you all right?' I shook his arm.

Slowly his face turned to me. 'They're all out there,' he said. 'I couldn't get them in.' He looked down at himself. 'I can't move,' he said. 'I'll just have to stay here. I might get shot but it doesn't matter. You go, though – back to the trench.' His eyes narrowed. 'I don't – forgive me; who are you? You're not in my platoon, are you?'

Fear twisted my insides. I had seen Sandy upset before but not – not actually *mad*. Or was he, like Mam before she died, delirious? But no, he was calm – weirdly calm.

'I've come to bring you in,' I said in my head-girl voice, or perhaps in the voice of the soldier he had taken me for. I shoved Kit's bike into the hedge. I couldn't wheel it *and* handle Sandy. 'Come on.' I took his arm. 'Take a step.' I had seen many a woman drag her husband out of the Red Lion and up Eupatoria Street. One foot shifted – the slowest thing I had ever seen. 'And another,' I coaxed. It was half a mile to the house. We wouldn't be home till Christmas! But the act of walking seemed to release Sandy from his frozen grip. The next steps were easier, but as we reached the ruined cottage he said, in a distant, polite voice, 'It's so quiet. I don't think I know this sector.'

'We're nearly home,' I said. But was it *home* to Sandy? 'Cliffside House?' I grabbed at his other arm, and made him look at me. 'It's me, Stella. Remember?' I shook him as if I could jerk him back to reality. 'The war's over. Everything's all right.' A lie. But what was I supposed to say? Was truth best? 'You were on your way to Helen's funeral,' I said gently. 'But – I don't think you can have made it?'

His good eye searched my face. His was bone-white in the dusk. He seemed to come back from wherever he'd been. He reached out and touched the nearest bit of cottage wall.

'I didn't go,' he said slowly. 'I let her down. I let everybody down. Same as in France.'

'You *didn't*.'

His features distorted in anger. 'What would *you* know?' he spat out. 'You weren't *there*. You're only a girl.'

Saliva landed on my cheek. My compassion flailed and died. 'Don't you ever,' I said, 'call me *only a girl*.'

I pulled away, wiped my cheek and began to stride up the loaning, rage and hurt surging, head splintered by thoughts. I was only trying to *help*! God knows it wasn't easy – all these men full of rage and guilt and horror; what were we *supposed* to do? Even Rose – who loved Charlie so much she'd let it overcome her principles about the war – *I don't know what to say to him.*

This was the corner where the house came into view. I'd never approached it in the dusk before. It looked cosy, lights shining in the drawing-room window and in Kit's. The window above, Sandy's, was in darkness. I thought of all the times I had seen him standing at that window, looking over the sea.

I let her down.

I'd let Mam down. And if anyone had tried to reassure

me that I hadn't, anyone who hadn't been through that nightmare with us, I'd have been angry too.

I spun round and ran back.

He hadn't moved.

'I'm sorry.' I touched his hand briefly. 'You're right; I wasn't there. I just don't know what to say.'

His mouth worked as if he was trying out a foreign language. 'I – we were – it was hopeless,' he said. 'I should have given the order to retreat. I knew that. Save whoever I could. But I froze. Couldn't move. Or speak. Hardly anyone came back. It was my fault.' He looked me properly in the face. 'I killed them.' His whole body started to shake. 'I killed them all.' His knees sagged. He gave a dry, retching moan, half-collapsed forwards on to the cottage wall, and started to cry, his face buried in his arms.

I'd hardly ever seen an adult cry, and never a man. It was the violent kind, that racks your whole body. His sobs punctured the still dusk, and a late seagull shrieked. I stood behind him and, nervous at first and then more confident, slid my arm across his heaving shoulders.

His hat tipped off, landed the wrong side of the wall. Wind ruffled his hair and maybe the cold feel of it, or just the fact that you *can't* keep crying forever, seemed to rouse him. He straightened up, dashed an arm across his face. 'S-sorry,' he choked out. His face was marbled with tears and mucus, and red-raw where he'd dragged the rough tweed of his sleeve across it. He scrabbled in his coat pockets, looking for a handkerchief, I supposed, but without success, maybe because his hands shook so much.

I took out my own; luckily it was clean. I was going to hand it to him, but instead I wiped his face the way Mam used to wipe mine when I was a child. He said, 'Thank you,' in a small, formal voice and went back to the scrabbling, eventually digging out a battered packet of cigarettes.

When he had lit one, and was leaning back against the wall smoking it, things felt more normal. The smell of the smoke, hanging in the cold still air, was reassuring.

I leaned right over the wall – Nancy would have been scandalised at the way it made my skirt ride up – and retrieved his hat. I brushed it against my coat and held it out. 'Do you want to tell me about today?' I said. 'You don't have to,' I added. 'We can just go home. You must be exhausted.'

'I haven't gone anywhere to *get* exhausted,' he said, with an effort at a laugh that ended in the dry rasp of a caught breath.

'Crying wears you out,' I said. 'And I don't suppose you've had much practice. Not being *only a girl*.'

He darted me a sideways glance and concentrated on smoking. When he'd finished he tossed the end away and sighed. 'I don't want to go in yet,' he said. 'Don't want to see anyone.'

I looked at my wristwatch. 'If we leave it about twenty minutes,' I said, 'they'll all be at dinner and you can slip upstairs in peace. I can distract them with tales of my honest toil on the farm. They won't expect you to dinner, will they?'

He shook his head. 'I imagined I'd stay in Belfast.'

'For ever?'

He shrugged. 'What does "for ever" mean? I didn't think beyond the funeral. I *meant* to go, Stella. I know how important funerals are. Even in France, if we could manage it. We couldn't always. There wasn't always anything to bury.'

'I know,' I said. 'I mean – about funerals. Mam's – well, it was horrible. Seeing her go down into that hole' – I cleared my throat; it wouldn't help if *I* started blubbing – 'was the worst thing ever. But I wouldn't have wanted to miss it. Still, you'll be able to go and see Helen's grave, won't you? That'll be *something*.'

'*If* I ever get further than the crossroads.'

'But you haven't been *anywhere* for so long,' I said gently. 'How could you think you'd suddenly be able to go as far as Belfast?'

'I don't know.' He shook his head. 'I had to force myself to take every step, and my head was spinning, and I couldn't breathe – I thought I was having a heart attack. I stopped to try to get a breath and – and then – I couldn't move again.' He twisted his mouth as if at something disgusting. 'I told you – I let people down.'

'No.'

'I couldn't even go and post the letter myself,' he burst out. 'And that time I was meant to look for you – I only pretended.'

'It doesn't matter.'

'Of course it bloody matters!' He sounded close to tears

again. 'Helen won't have got my letter in time. She died not *knowing* – thinking I didn't care about her.'

Like Mam and Rose.

He was right. No matter how quickly the letter got to Belfast, it couldn't have been before she died. I imagined Helen's mother picking it up from the doormat along with letters of condolence. A bit like people who must have got telegrams about their sons and sweethearts being killed, while they were celebrating the Armistice. Everything overlapped with everything else. Everything was mixed up.

'You can start trying now,' I suggested. 'Go a bit further each day.' And eventually, I thought, end up at Charlie and Rose's where hard work would finish off the cure. 'I'll help.'

'Stella!' He pulled the brim of his hat further down so his face was in shadow. 'Why do you always think you can *fix* everything? Some things – you just can't.'

And he stomped off ahead of me, back to the house.

26

I forgot about Kit's bicycle and she found it in the hedge next morning, with brambles tangled in the rear spokes and bird mess on the handlebars. The reaction was predictable.

'I don't know how you could be so irresponsible,' Nancy said, and I mumbled something about stopping to do something. She must have thought I had had to go to the lavatory behind a hedge or something, which was mortifying, but I knew Sandy would hate me to tell her about finding him in that state. I thought of making up some story about finding one of the Mahon children in distress and stopping to help, but she'd have panicked about germs. I couldn't win.

Sandy went back to being a ghost in the attic. Nancy or I carried his meals up. He ate little, and spoke less, preferring us to leave the tray outside.

'Grief,' Nancy said, returning to the kitchen one evening with a barely-touched rabbit stew. 'When Daddy died I couldn't eat for weeks. Only thing I could fancy was fruit cake.'

'When Mam died,' I remembered, 'all I could do was drink tea.'

'Still.' She frowned. 'It was only his *cousin*. And he must have suffered worse losses than that – I mean, friends and comrades.'

'I think she was more like a sister,' I said. 'And maybe – well, all the losses pile up. And you can only take so much before you crack.' Not just Sandy but the whole country. How much grief could we all take?

I supposed I'd thought – hoped – that breaking down would be a sort of turning point for Sandy. Like starting to recover from a fever once you'd passed the crisis. Despite what he'd said about not *fixing* him, I couldn't help planning ways to get him out, easy routes, milestones: to the bend in the loaning, to the oak tree, to the red gate, to the old cottage. Further and easier each day until we were working together at the farm, and he and Charlie miraculously mended each other.

But not if Sandy never left his room! And people *didn't* always weather the crisis and start to recover. Sometimes they died.

I walked to the farm one day, setting off early in the morning, but by the time I arrived I was too tired to be much use. Rose had got bigger, and slower, and her back clearly hurt; she and Charlie watched each other with identical worried creases on their foreheads. The way their faces cleared when they saw me made me feel important and determined. Even though what I really wanted was to sit in the kitchen and drink tea and talk about Mam and the old days.

'Could you muck out a stall?' Charlie asked.

'Of course,' I said loftily. I barely knew what a stall was, but it couldn't be much worse than the hen-house.

'I'm letting the old mare out today,' he said. 'She's had six weeks' rest. If she's not sound now, I reckon that's the end of her.'

I followed him into the dark, smelly stable and tried not to breathe in while he untied the mare and backed her out of the stall. She was black and white with deep hollows above her eyes and huge splaying hooves that I kept well away from. Charlie led her out into a scrubby paddock. Rose was waiting at the gate, a basket of eggs over her arm. Charlie opened the gate and the old mare barged in, lifted her head and smelt the air, then, almost before he'd pulled off her halter, trotted stiffly up the hill, tail in the air, and plunged her nose into the grass. I turned to Charlie, smiling, sure he would be pleased, but he and Rose were both frowning.

'Lame as a duck,' Charlie said. 'That's that then.' He flung the halter over his shoulder and limped back to the yard, Rose and I following.

'Maybe more rest?' Rose suggested, but Charlie shook his head.

'If it was going to heal, it'd have healed by now. No, that's the end of her.'

'You won't send her for *meat*?' I asked, with a horrified memory of *Black Beauty*.

'Can't feed a useless horse. And can't afford to buy another one.' He hung up the halter and went off up the yard. I looked at Rose in despair.

'He doesn't mean it,' she said. 'He's just worried. She wasn't great at pulling the old cart, but she was better than nothing. We've managed without going to town for the last six weeks, but we can't manage forever. There's things we need.'

'Nancy has a car,' I said. 'She could take you into town.'

'Och, I don't think Nancy would be wanting that,' Rose said.

'Other neighbours?'

She shook her head. 'Old Mrs O'Hare's all on her own and the Agnews – well, they don't really bother.'

I set to mucking out the stall. The old mare may not have been much good at walking, but her bowels had been active. By the time I had raked up five wheelbarrow-loads of the stinking straw, and trundled it to the midden, my muscles were shrieking and I felt filthy. But the stall, swilled out with water and Lysol, shone. I gave it a last sweep with the broom, and pushed my sweaty hair out of my eyes. There was no sign of Charlie, and Rose was in the house. I wasn't sure what they'd want me to do next but being so dirty I thought I should stick to outside work. I wasn't exactly enjoying it, but I felt Land-girlish and noble. I put the wheelbarrow and brush back in a shed that was cluttered with old buckets stacked anyhow, and piles of rusted machinery. And that's when I saw the bicycle.

It wasn't new and shining like Kit's or even shabby but

decent like the one I still hoped Nancy might buy me for Christmas. It was rusted in patches, and the tyres were flat, *and* it was a man's bike, with a crossbar. I didn't know if it would ever be rideable, or if a girl *could* ride a bike like that, but it was no use to anyone else. Rose had already said that cycling was one of the things Charlie couldn't manage with one leg, and she was hardly likely to try in her condition. I wheeled the machine out of the shed and into the damp cold air. Even wheeling, it felt twice as heavy as Kit's, but it had wheels. It had to be worth a try.

Charlie laughed when he saw it; I had never heard him laugh before. 'Would you honestly give it a go?' he asked.

Up went my chin. 'Certainly,' I said. 'If it can be made rideable, I'll ride it. It took me well over an hour to walk here today,' I explained, 'and I'll have to leave soon because of it getting dark. But if I had *this* …'

He turned it over. 'It's sound enough,' he said, 'and probably not as old as it looks. It must have been Joe's.' He wiped away some of the dust.

'Rose's brother?'

'Hmmm.'

'Can I borrow it, then?'

'Take it and welcome. Only don't expect too much.'

'I always do!' I told him.

As I walked home, wheeling it beside me – Charlie had pumped up the tyres and wiped off the worst of the dirt, but I wasn't confident enough to try riding it for the first time out on the mountain road – I had another hope. Sandy was good with bikes – he'd known what to do when I scratched

Kit's. He could help me restore it, give me some tips on riding with a crossbar – I would have to do something inventive and undignified with my skirt, and then, surely, he would start to behave like a normal person? I imagined us riding the bicycle up to the farm, Sandy pedalling, me balancing on the seat. It was a sturdy old bike, it could probably take us both.

I took Sandy's dinner tray up and asked him straight out would he help me restore an old bicycle. And he barely looked up from his book and said, 'No.'

So over the next few days I did it myself. I wasn't sure how safe it was, and I got gallons of oil over myself, and I fell off three times learning to ride it, once quite hard and putting holes in my knees like I used to do as a child falling in the street, but I did it.

After that, I went to the farm whenever I liked.

I knew Nancy disapproved, but she didn't actually forbid me. I think she was relieved not to have me hanging around agitating for action.

At dinner I was always tired, which Nancy probably liked, as it made me less inclined to contribute to the conversation, which was all about the end of the war, and the flu raging harder. Schools and public places had closed for a fortnight. Even the Mountainview Hotel in Cuanbeg closed, which Miss McKay said had never happened in her lifetime. 'It feels,' she said, 'like the end of the world.'

She gave a little laugh, as if she knew she was being foolish, but I couldn't help shivering.

27

But the world didn't end, and soon the papers were full of something else – the forthcoming general election on 14 December. Only a couple of weeks away! It was hard not to feel sad as well as happy that women – at least women over thirty – would be voting for the first time. This is what Mam had fought for, and she wasn't alive to vote.

'Are you excited about voting?' I asked Nancy one day when she was serving the chops.

Mrs Phillips tutted. 'Really, what a topic for the dinner table!'

'It's a very suitable topic,' I said. 'We're all women, and citizens.'

'*You're* a child,' Mrs Phillips said, 'and would do well to remember that.'

'That's unfair,' Miss McKay said. 'Stella has been doing the work of a grown woman.'

I smiled at her. 'Are *you* looking forward to voting for the first time, Miss McKay?' I asked her.

'But it isn't the first time,' she said. 'I have exercised my right to vote in local elections ever since that was granted.' She sounded proud.

'Good for you.' I helped myself to turnip.

'Though,' Miss McKay went on, 'living in rooms now, I won't be eligible. A woman has to be a householder to vote.'

'Or married to one.' Mrs Phillips wrinkled her nose. '*I* have no wish to vote,' she said, as if voting was some especially disgusting thing. 'And my father the judge was very much against it. As was my dear Cedric.'

'Against *voting*?' I asked. 'You mean they didn't believe in *democracy*? Were they *anarchists*? How exciting!'

'Stella!' Nancy said, and Mrs Phillips gathered her scarves and said that I knew perfectly well what she meant and that it was hoydens like me who gave womanhood a bad name.

Kit said, 'Good for Stella! I wish *I'd* known more about politics when I was her age. I'd certainly vote if I were old enough. It's unfair that we can't.' It was the nicest she'd been to me since I left her bicycle in the hedge.

'It's so the electorate won't be too skewed in favour of the female vote,' Nancy said. 'So many men have been lost. If they let women vote at twenty-one, like men, the electorate would be unbalanced.'

I snorted. 'The electorate has been skewed in favour of *men* forever,' I pointed out. 'Nobody seemed to have any problem with that – apart from suffragists, of course.'

'But this is the first time the suffrage has been extended

to all *men* over twenty-one,' Nancy said. 'We just need to be patient a little longer.'

'I don't see why,' I muttered, at the same time as Kit said, 'It's always *women* who have to be patient. It's not fair I shouldn't vote when my brother can, and he's younger than me.'

'Your brother has served his country,' Mrs Phillips said.

Kit jerked her head up. 'And what do you think *I'm* doing?'

I joined in. 'That's one reason why I don't agree that women have been given the vote as a sort of thank-you for their war work,' I said. 'Because most of the ones who've done that – like Kit here, and munitions workers and tram conductors and Land Girls' – I had developed a great fellow feeling for Land Girls – 'are *young* women who *still* can't vote.'

'And what's the other reason, dear?' Miss McKay asked.

'Well, it's denying that the suffragettes' direct action brought results,' I said. 'They won't admit that.'

'Because it's nonsense!' Mrs Phillips said. 'Unwomanly carry-on! No better than hooligans.'

'My mam was not a hooligan!'

'Ladies!' Nancy said. 'Let's not descend into a brawl.'

'I hope *you're* planning to vote?' I demanded. 'Seeing you're the only person here actually eligible. In Mam's memory if for no other reason?'

She gave a little laugh. 'Your mother would doubtless turn in her grave to see me vote for Irwin McAndrew,' she said. 'She called him an odious imperialist.'

'Irwin McAndrew is a good loyal unionist gentleman,' Mrs Phillips said. 'And he's served this constituency for nigh on twenty years.'

'He nearly didn't get back in in 1910,' Miss McKay said. 'The Home Rulers were starting to make their presence felt.'

The conversation took a slightly different turn. At home, it had been about whether you were Conservative or Liberal, or, like Mam and me, Labour. Here in Ireland it seemed to be about tribe or religion more than class. I remembered Sandy saying there would be bloodshed before the whole Home Rule question was sorted out. As they all started to argue I was mortified to realise that I didn't really understand it all. If only Sandy wasn't being so distant and shut-away: he seemed to know a fair amount about it. I took to reading the paper more carefully – since the Armistice Kit brought it home most days – and learned that Sinn Féin, who wanted an independent Ireland, completely free of Britain, were mounting a huge campaign to get elected, and that the Irish Parliamentary Party, who believed in Home Rule but were much more moderate, had agreed in most places not to stand against the Sinn Féin candidate.

* * *

'Which means,' Rose explained, the next time I visited, 'that Sinn Féin will have a huge majority and then declare an Irish republic.' She sounded very pleased about this, and I must admit it sounded exciting.

'It won't be that simple,' Charlie said. For once he wasn't working; he had slipped on some ice in the yard, and come down hard on his back. He would have to go out soon to milk the cows, but for now he was resting in the kitchen. 'Not in Ulster, anyway. Too many places with a unionist majority.'

'What about round here?' I remembered the talk at dinner at home.

'Well, like a lot of places, it's divided,' Rose said. 'The unionists have always managed to get in, but there's been a rise in nationalist feeling since the Rising.'

'*And* conscription,' Charlie put in. 'That was the worst mistake the British government made – trying to *force* Irishmen to join up.'

'*You* volunteered,' I said.

'More fool me.' He looked down at his leg and saw me following his glance. 'Not just that,' he said. 'But round our way in Belfast – it's real diehard republican. I got spat at in the street for wearing the king's uniform. Called a traitor to Ireland.'

'Not by me,' Rose said, and handed him a cup of tea.

'No. But that's one reason we came here. To be anonymous. And quiet.'

Rose gave a little shiver. 'The baby moved,' she said, but I guessed that it wasn't just that. She was like me; she didn't like quiet.

'At least you can vote!' I reminded her. 'You're over thirty and a householder. You must be glad about that. It's not enough,' I added. 'There's a nurse living at Cliffside, and it's a *scandal* that she can't vote, but at least it's a start. Mam ...' I stopped, took a sip of tea even though it was still too hot, and coughed.

Rose stretched out her hand to me. 'I know,' she said.

'She had this plan,' I said. Somehow talking about Mam wasn't as painful with Rose. 'Of course, she didn't know *when* the election would be, but whenever it was, she was going to get all the local women who were eligible and make sure they knew how to vote and where to go and all that. She and her friends – remember Maud? And Sarah? – planned to hire a charabanc and go round all day, collecting women, taking them to the polling station.'

I had offered to help by typing out leaflets to tell women how to place their ballot. Lil and Sadie too. They weren't bothered about politics, but they'd have done it to help me and because Lil said it sounded a right laugh. It would have been a marvellous day: we would have forgotten that it was only a partial victory and celebrated what women had won. I had a stab of pain to think that this would still be happening, but without Mam and without me. I'd be stuck here in the middle of nowhere, with a crowd of old women who didn't even *care*.

'Rose,' I said suddenly. 'How will *you* get to the polling station?'

Rose and Charlie exchanged glances.

'We'll sort something out,' Charlie said. 'If we'd a new horse ...'

'There's no money for a horse,' Rose said. 'It doesn't matter. There'll be other elections.'

'Not like this one!' I argued. 'It'll never be the first time again! Rose – you went to *prison* for the right to vote! You nearly died!'

Charlie set his cup down. 'The cows'll not milk themselves,' he said. I could see he was in more discomfort than usual as he straightened his back, and made for the door. A gust of icy air came in when he opened it, and even after he had closed it behind him, the chill stayed in the room.

'Don't go on about it,' Rose said. 'He hates the fact that he can't give me things. That he can't even bring me into town to vote.' She stood up and tidied away the cups, clattering the china more than usual. 'I'd walk to the polling station if I could. But I can't get to the end of the lane these days without being out of breath.' She placed a hand on her belly. 'And I can't risk hurting the baby. There's been enough loss.'

'But how can you say it doesn't matter!'

'Of course it matters.' Her voice was hoarse and fierce. 'It breaks my heart not to be one of the first women to vote, when I've given so much for the cause. But it breaks my heart more to see Charlie worried. He nearly died too.' She lifted the pail and poured water into the sink. 'Och, you'll understand when you're older.'

I cycled home, disappointed in Rose for the first time.

You'll understand when you're older! I didn't see how I could ever feel older, or more hopeless, than I did now.

And then, turning into the driveway at Cliffside, skirting round the old Wolseley-Siddeley, I had the best idea I had ever had, in a lifetime of really quite good ideas. Rose *would* vote. I could make it happen.

28

I ran Nancy to ground in Mrs Phillips's room. The door was open and she was wiping down the paintwork with a damp cloth.

'She was complaining the dust made her cough,' she said.

'Can she not do that herself? It's not like she's got anything else to do except annoy people.'

'Don't be silly.' She wiped a damp lock of hair out of her eyes. 'It's what she pays for. And without Minnie ...'

'*I* would have done it.'

'When? You're hardly ever here.'

I bit my lip.

Nancy wrung out her cloth into her bucket. It looked awkward in her hands, and I wondered if, like Rose, like so many people, she felt she was living a life she hadn't been prepared for. 'Mrs Phillips is a good tenant,' she said. 'And she knows all sorts of people who might come in the summer.'

'Ugh, I hope they don't if they're anything like her!'

'Stella!'

I remembered I was meant to be asking a favour. I explained. Nancy listened, but frowned as she wiped the cloth over the broad windowsill. 'Rose wouldn't want *me* interfering.'

'She would! She's *longing* to vote. She's devoted her whole life to winning the right. She of all people *deserves* …'

'If you really believe in universal suffrage,' Nancy said, 'then you should believe that *everyone* deserves to vote.'

'You know what I mean.'

'Is this for Rose – or for Peggy?'

'Both.' I told her about Mam's plans for election day in Manchester. 'I want to help,' I said. 'To make it happen. Even for one woman. I know it's not much. It's tiny.' I shook my head at the frustration of *how* tiny. 'But it's all I can do. And it isn't tiny to Rose. But I can't do it without your help. I mean, *I* can't drive the car.'

'Given your tendency to take vehicles which don't belong to you, and the way you treat them, I'm glad you can't,' Nancy said drily, but with the trace of a smile on her lips. Then the smile faded. 'Oh – hello, Mrs Phillips. I'm sorry; I thought I'd have finished by now. I won't be a minute.'

Mrs Phillips stood in the doorway. She looked at me and sniffed as if I smelt bad. I probably did; I was usually sweaty when I came back from the farm.

'Is there no escape from this vulgar talk of polling stations and politics?' she said.

I was about to say that we'd been having a private conversation but strictly speaking it was her room, so I nobly forbore, and said, pleasantly, 'Nancy's taking my friend Rose to the polling station on election day.'

'Indeed?' She wrinkled her forehead but not as if she were genuinely puzzled, more sort of acting puzzled. 'That rebel person? I imagine she intends to vote' – she swallowed as if it hurt to force out the words – 'Sinn Féin?'

'Of course.' I remembered the spark in Rose's eyes when she'd talked about an Irish republic.

'Miss Graham,' Mrs Phillips said to Nancy, 'I sincerely hope you would not contemplate facilitating the vote of a – a rebel? And a jailbird?' She pressed on before Nancy could say anything: 'If my poor Cedric … I came here believing this was a decent loyal establishment. I've recommended you to the dear Reverend Mehaffey himself!' She wafted her hand in front of her nose as if she were about to faint in horror. 'Why, your own father – such a good friend of my father the judge – would spin in his grave!'

I waited for Nancy to say that this was her house and she would give a lift to anyone she damn well pleased. But she straightened up from cleaning the sill and said, 'Well, Stella *hoped* I could help her friend. But I'm inclined to agree that it wouldn't be suitable. Sorry, Stella.'

I was so angry I turned and stomped downstairs. I went outside and banged about in the garden in the drizzling dusk, trying not to let my rage bubble over into babyish tears. How could she be so small-minded! And so weak!

I wished I could take the car myself. Carnap it, in the early morning, before anyone was about. I saw myself proudly pulling up at the polling station, with a VOTES

FOR WOMEN banner draped over the car and Rose sitting proud and grateful beside me. The streets would be full of suffragettes, and they would see us coming and run behind the car waving banners and cheering ... and then somehow Mam was there too, and we were back in Manchester, and I shook the image and some stupid tears away at the same time.

I strode along the loaning to the point where you could see the sea. Its sulky pewter matched my mood, but didn't calm me, just churned me up more. I would have to get away. The fresh air and wide spaces stifled me more than the smoky narrow streets I'd grown up in. I could get a job in Belfast – in an office, or even as a maid. If only I'd disobeyed Nancy the day of Helen's funeral, and gone with Sandy. I was sure *I'd* have got him on the train; and then I'd have gone to the city and not come back. There was nothing for me here. Just as there had been nothing for Mam. And Mam had run away. All the way to England with me safely inside her. And Rose by her side.

Except ... I frowned, dug my hands into the pockets of my cardigan. I didn't want to leave Rose before the baby was born. I was looking forward to the baby; to new life. And they relied on me now. Even if I couldn't get Rose to the polling station, I could do other things – cleaning the hen-house, doing the heavier work indoors. She would need me more, not less, as the baby's birth grew closer.

Approaching the old cottage, I saw a lumbering, awkward figure that reminded me of the evening I'd met Sandy here. But as it came closer I realised it was Minnie, bundled into a big shawl and with a child clinging to her skirt. She had another one straddling her hip; too old to be the new baby but too young to toddle.

'Hello, Minnie!' I called. She looked up and nodded, then carried on her way, murmuring to the children. I was glad she hadn't stopped. I wouldn't have known what to say. Even though my mother had died in the same way as Minnie's, I knew I was a million times luckier.

I decided to be silent at dinner. Nancy would think I was sulking, but there was no way I could open my mouth without fighting or – much worse – crying, so I kept quiet. I toyed with my dinner, and tried not to get annoyed when Mrs Phillips, noticing my lack of interest in food, speculated loudly about the state of my health and hoped that I was not coming down with flu. A number of the clergy had died from it. They were, of course, so vulnerable. She hoped her own dear Reverend Mehaffey would escape. She prayed for him every night and morning, to be sure, but was prayer enough in these times? And poor Mr Irwin McAndrew, the local MP, had we seen in the paper that his son had succumbed? Oh yes, only twelve, he was. 'Though I'm sure,' she said, 'that it will encourage people to vote for him.'

'Hardly an electoral advantage he would have wished for,' Nancy said.

'He'll get in anyway,' Miss McKay pronounced. 'Sinn Féin's never been strong around here, and it seems they're fielding some young chap from Dublin that nobody's ever heard of. They must know he doesn't have a hope.'

'Gosh, Miss McKay, you sound knowledgeable,' Kit said. I tried not to feel annoyed. *I* was meant to be the political one.

'The nationalists came a close second here in 1910,' Miss McKay went on. 'And it's not like they've agreed not to stand as they have done in most other places to let Sinn Féin have a free run at it. That will split the Catholic vote. A vote for Sinn Féin in this constituency is a wasted vote. You might as well vote for a giraffe.'

'Jolly good,' Mrs Phillips said. 'My Cedric would be pleased.'

I couldn't help giving Nancy a sideways look.

She came to my bedroom later that evening, and hovered in a very irritating way. I kept pretending to read *Middlemarch*. She picked up the little picture of Winfred Carney, though I don't suppose she knew who she was.

'All right,' she said. 'I'll do it. I don't agree with Rose's politics. Not one bit. But – well, she stood by Peggy when nobody in her own family did.'

She was doing it because it was hopeless. Because she believed Rose's vote for Sinn Féin would make no difference whatsoever. But at least she was doing it.

'I wish you'd said this in front of Mrs Phillips,' I said. 'She should know she can't bully you in your own house.'

'Well, there's no need to make a big song and dance of everything, is there?' Nancy said.

I sighed. A big song and dance was exactly what I wanted.

29

When I told Rose she cried. Not actual sobbing, but her eyes glittered and she grasped my hands the way she'd done the first day I came. It was washing day; the kitchen steamed with wet sheets and her hands were damp and warm.

'This means – you'll never know how much,' she said. 'To Charlie too.'

'Charlie?'

'It'll be his first time as well.'

Of course Charlie was a householder since he'd taken over the farm. But in any case non-householders could vote now too – as long as they were male.

'I'll run out and tell him,' I said, 'and I'll clean out the hens while I'm there.'

Charlie was more grudging in his thanks, but with a supreme effort of empathy I realised that his pride must be dented: that I, a stranger really, could do this thing for his wife that he couldn't.

They had resigned themselves to the *Belfast Telegraph*. Rose pored over any old copies I brought with enthusiasm for election news.

'Winifred is standing in Belfast!' she said one day.

'Blimey! Will she get in? I wish a woman was standing *here*.'

Rose looked at the article. 'Victoria ward,' she said. She made a face. 'East Belfast. Safe unionist seat.' She sighed. 'She hasn't got a hope. Not like Countess Markievicz in Dublin. *She'll* get in all right.'

'But there must be lots of women – factory workers and the like – who'd vote for Winifred because of her trade unionism. I mean, she stands for workers' rights and –'

'Of course she does. But she was in the GPO in 1916, and then imprisoned by the British government. Unionist women will see that before they see what she's done for working women.'

'But that's awful!' Instantly I wanted to go to Belfast and help Winifred to campaign. I imagined myself standing on a soapbox, shouting *Vote for Carney! Vote for a woman!*

Rose shrugged. 'It's how it is here. Being a unionist or a nationalist trumps anything else.'

'Maybe that'll change,' I suggested.

'Maybe.' Rose looked sad for a moment, then grinned and said, 'But at least I can vote. Thanks to you.'

'And Nancy.'

'Yes. She never liked me, you know. So it's doubly kind of her.'

'Why did she not like you?'

Rose shrugged. 'Och, you know. Ancient history. I – we – were a bad influence on her sister.'

'We?'

'Well …' She turned the page of the paper and seemed to be studying it very closely though it was only an advertisement for corsets, which couldn't be of much interest to her just now. 'Me and Joe, my brother, you know. The three of us were pals.'

'Mam never mentioned Joe. Only you.'

'Ah, well then.' Her voice was dismissive.

'What happened him?'

'He died. Not in the war. A long time ago. He was hit by a streetcar in New York. He went there when – about the same time your mam went to England.'

Mam always said my father had been killed in an accident in America. *Joe – was – my father!*

I didn't say it out loud. I felt I'd been dim not to have worked it out before, but Rose's face told me she didn't want to say any more. Why had Mam never told me? Was she waiting for me to be old enough to understand? I was old enough now.

I looked at Rose's belly. If I was right, that was my cousin in there. And Rose was my aunt every bit as much as Nancy. I wanted to shriek and hug her and tell her I had worked it out, but –

There's no need to make a big song and dance out of everything.

'Will you tell me about him some day?' I asked.

'Some day.'

I had to be careful not to spend too much time with Rose and Charlie. I didn't want to make Nancy jealous, especially when she was doing me such a favour. I made myself useful and didn't say too much about the farm. I certainly didn't tell her that I thought I knew who my father had been.

I missed Sandy. It had been all very well having him hide away in his room before I'd known him. Now I hated seeing the shut door, the barely touched trays, the blank window. Every day I thought, *Today might be the day he starts to feel better, wants to come back to the world again,* but every day I was wrong.

'Grief takes time,' Kit said one day when she caught me looking up at his window when I was meant to be tidying the garden after a storm had brought down some leaves and small branches.

'I know.' I blushed in case she thought I was sweet on him, and then blushed more because the first blush might have suggested that I *was*.

'Some of the men at Sunny View are the same,' she said. 'Closed in on themselves. And some are angry. And some cry. And some' – she gave a little laugh – 'are cheerful and teasing, even when they're sitting there with no arms or no legs. I suppose we're all different.'

'Will you stay here, now the war's over?' I asked.

'Yes,' she said. 'I don't have a great deal to go home for. My chap was killed at Gallipoli.'

'I didn't know.'

'No. So I might as well stay. At least I'm needed. Talking of which, I must go. We're short-staffed again. Two orderlies off with flu.'

Flu at Sunny View! I didn't let myself think about it. I turned back to my work. The pile of dirty old leaves looked disgusting. I heaped the last forkful on to the wheelbarrow and pushed it down to the compost heap, which looked even worse, all wet and dark and smelly. I tipped the barrow up and saw the newer leaves mix with the old ones, brittle brown amongst slimy black, and then, glinting in the dark mess, something bright, like one star in a black sky. A threepenny bit. I picked it up and rubbed the muck off with my glove. It was too tarnished to shine much, but it seemed a tiny spark of hope.

30

As December sulked along, the election was only days away. I had ringed the date – Saturday 14 December – on a calendar and crossed off the days. The time after the fourteenth looked very blank. There would be helping at home and at the farm, of course, but it seemed awfully – little. I wanted the world to change. *I* wanted to change it.

The day before the election, I washed the car to make it gleam for its important mission. I felt modern and dashing, shining up the headlamps. If only, I thought, giving it a last polish, you weren't so terrifying.

Later the rain came and I chopped carrots in the kitchen while Nancy peeled potatoes. This wasn't anything like such hard work, but much duller and less modern. Rain battered at the window and everything looked grey apart from the bright orange carrots.

'I was thinking about tomorrow,' I said. 'You don't need me to go with you, do you?'

'What? But – you're so excited about the election.'

'I thought I could walk into town and meet you there.

I'd still get to see Rose go and vote. And you of course. I'd enjoy the walk.'

'Ah!' She nodded wisely. 'Are you worried about being sick again? I'll go very carefully.'

'Maybe a bit.' I blushed at my knife. She didn't know how scared I was. She probably didn't imagine anyone could be so silly. Especially anyone like me. I changed the subject. 'Isn't it your day for Sunny View?' I asked. 'Oh – I suppose you're not going because of the flu.'

She tidied the peelings into a bucket. 'Yes,' she said. 'And also' – she grimaced – 'my back's sore, and I've got the drive tomorrow. Thought I'd have a wee rest today.'

'Too much housework,' I said, pushing away a slight but definite dread. 'I thought Sissy Mahon was supposed to be starting?'

'She hasn't turned up.'

'Will I go and ask at the cottage? Maybe she forgot.'

Nancy sighed. 'No, Stella. There must be illness there again. I don't want *you* catching anything.'

Since the flu at Sunny View, Nancy had set up a washing station at the back door, and made Kit change out of her uniform and wash in Lysol before she came any further into the house, hanging her uniform up in the dank little passage outside the scullery.

'It's damp!' Kit had complained the first morning. 'If you ask me, that's more likely to give me flu!'

But Nancy was adamant. And Mrs Phillips, whose scarf was permanently round her mouth these days, though it didn't stop her talking, was even more so. The flu was a wolf stalking the country, huffing and puffing, and we were the little pigs barricading our houses against it.

But even the strongest house wasn't proof against this enemy. That evening Nancy didn't come to dinner.

'She's lying down,' Miss McKay said. 'Nothing to worry about.' She smiled at me and gave me much too much dinner.

I stared at my plate, a ball of fear swelling in my throat. I tried to force down a piece of carrot, sick with dread. I scraped away a bit of skin that had stuck to my potato, thought of Nancy peeling them. *My back's sore. I have to drive tomorrow.*

Was this going to be how our election day would end up?

After a dinner that nobody had been able to do much with, Miss McKay, who looked older than usual, her skin like the underside of a dry leaf, said, 'Take your aunt a cup of tea, and then go and look in your room. I've made you a wee surprise.'

Nancy's room was in semi-darkness, the curtains closed. She wasn't in bed, but lying on top of it with a crocheted blanket over her. I hovered in the doorway.

'Don't look so scared,' Nancy said. She struggled into a sitting position. 'Is that tea? Good.'

'Do you have flu?' I jerked out, setting the tray on her bedside table.

Nancy frowned and with a burst of hope I remembered asking that before, when it turned out to be women's troubles.

'I'm fine. Touch of headache. I get them when I overdo things. Don't worry about me. I'm going to have an early night and I'll be fine for driving the election bus in the morning.'

'Promise?' I asked childishly.

'Promise. Now pour me out that tea before it gets stewed.'

In my bedroom I found, folded on the bed, a new scarf, in soft thick wool, purple, green and white stripes – suffragette colours. I knew it was for wearing to the polling station tomorrow. I thought of Miss McKay's stiff, kind old fingers making it in secret, and wrapped it round me at once, for comfort and maybe for luck.

31

I slept badly. Every shift and creak of the house, every owl's shriek, every scrape of a branch against the window made me start and tense myself for more sinister noises. I remembered lying awake in Eupatoria Street listening to Mam coughing and choking in the next room. Forcing myself to get up and go in. The blood frothing at her lips; her face turning blue; her hands scrabbling at her throat as she fought for the breath that wouldn't come –

Was that a cough? Downstairs? I sat up and lit my bedside lamp. But everything was quiet. Annoyingly, though, I now needed the lavatory. Cursing, I shrugged into my dressing gown, and crept down to the bathroom, only to arrive at the same time as Sandy, coming from downstairs. We both danced around a bit in discomfort – not needing-the-lav discomfort, just general embarrassment, because after days of not seeing each other and him being so mean about the bicycle it seemed an ignoble situation in which to meet. And it was the middle of the night.

'Ladies first,' he said.

I could have tilted my chin and told him not to be so old-fashioned but my need was quite urgent, so I said, 'Thank you, Captain Reid,' in a tone of the utmost coolness and went in to do what I had to do. I hoped he wouldn't be waiting when I got out – surely he would go and hover upstairs out of decency – but when I opened the door again, there he was. I held it open and went to walk past him.

'Please don't call me Captain Reid,' he said. 'I hate it.'

Cold moonlight at the landing window showed his face to be not just pale, but grey and sort of crumpled, like a very badly laundered sheet. Oh God! Maybe *he* was sickening too – he certainly looked far from healthy; probably we would all get it and die off, one by one, like that family I read about in the paper, who were all found dead in their beds in their own filth.

'Well, *I* hate people not helping me to fix my bike,' I said, because it was easier than saying what I was really worried about. 'And being my friend and then just *disappearing*.' I sounded about ten.

'I haven't gone anywhere.'

'You know what I mean,' I said crossly. And then something awful happened. I started to cry, horrible, snottery, gasping sobs, punctuated by words that made no sense: 'Nancy – all going to die – I know it.' Now I sounded about five.

'Stella!' He put his arm round me. He smelt smoky and indoorsy but his arm felt strong. 'What's wrong?'

'She – she didn't come to dinner. And she said her – her

155

back was sore.' Fresh sobs burst out. 'And then she said – a – a headache. But I know! I – I *know*.'

He gave me a little shake. 'You *don't*. And even if it is' – his face clouded – 'it doesn't mean she'll *die*. Most people don't. *I* didn't. *You* didn't.'

'My mam did. Helen did. Minnie's mam – thousands of people! *M-millions!*'

'But she mightn't.' He pulled out a handkerchief and handed it to me, and the gesture reminded me of when I'd been the one trying to do the comforting, and he'd been the one in a state. In books people cry romantically, but we both seemed prone to the unromantic kind. I took a shuddering breath and gave a rather disgusting sniff.

'Right,' Sandy said. He pulled me down beside him so we were both sitting on the top stair. '*If* Nancy has flu, we'll cope with it. We're luckier than most people. There's plenty of room, and she can afford a doctor.'

'The doctor won't come!' I wailed. 'There aren't enough to go round.'

'Well, we've a trained nurse in the house.'

'Not right now. She's on night duty.' My voice rose in a shriek. 'She's going to die, I know she is. It'll be like Mam all over again.'

'Stella!' He gave me another shake, a harder one. 'Stop it. This isn't like you.'

'What d'you mean?'

'You're never scared! You always see how things can be done. I bet you *anything* she hasn't got flu. And *if* she does, I bet she doesn't have it badly.'

'I haven't got anything to bet,' I said. 'And I'm scared of lots of things.'

I played with his handkerchief, and wondered why men got such large ones when they didn't cry anything like as much as women. His hand lay beside mine on the green carpet. The moonlight picked out the pale face of his wristwatch: nearly half past two. I yawned. And then froze as a cough split the night.

'Oh God!' I said, all my panic rushing back.

'It's only Mrs Phillips. She often coughs half the night. It's like living with the Brontës. Talking of which – you should get back to bed instead of sitting round in your nightclothes, even if you have teamed them with that very fetching scarf.'

32

I expected to wake early on election day, the way I used to at Christmas. I'd imagined dancing around impatiently, waiting for Nancy to finish breakfast, anxious to get going.

But nothing turned out that way.

For a start I overslept. After my conversation with Sandy I had fallen into fitful sleep, only to drop off properly close to dawn. By the time I woke, it was really late. I pulled open the curtains and saw that the day, though grey, was light; that meant that it must be close to nine. Breakfast would be nearly over; they would tease me for being late, and Mrs Phillips would say something sarky about me never changing the world if I couldn't even get out of my bed on time. But I would bear it with noble fortitude – if only Nancy was there, upright and healthy.

I dashed out of my room, and as soon as I got to the top of the stairs a stench of carbolic hit me. Nancy's bedroom door was open and Kit came out, still in her uniform.

Nancy won't like that, I thought; she likes her to change. And then the significance hit me.

'Oh God!' I said. 'Is she –?'

'Don't shriek,' Kit said quietly. 'She got up and fainted. I've just got her back to bed.'

My hand flew to my mouth. 'I *knew!* I –'

'Shh. I've hung a sheet over the doorway, soaked in carbolic. You're not to go in, Stella. Promise me?'

'But –'

'She's not too bad. Honestly. If she stays where she is and rests properly there's no reason on earth why she shouldn't get better. I'll look after her. I'm due a couple of days off.'

'The doctor?'

'If we need him we'll ask for him. But her temp's only up slightly. She shouldn't have tried to get up, but she kept insisting she couldn't let you down. I told her you'd understand.'

'Of course I do,' I said. 'As long as Nancy gets better it doesn't matter a bit.' I said it loudly, hoping she would hear from behind that strange billowing sheet that looked like a child's drawing of a ghost.

Miss McKay came up the stairs. 'Stella,' she said. 'Get dressed and come down for some porridge. Mrs Phillips is having hysterics in her room – she's convinced her hour has come. But I can trust *you* to be sensible.'

She said it like a warning.

The whole house felt hushed and strange. Nancy was safely in her bedroom, with the door closed, but the whiff of carbolic hung in the air.

I scuttled past on my way down to the breakfast I

couldn't face. Miss McKay stood over me as I ate it, though, and pretty much force-fed me.

'When you've had that, wrap up warm and go outside. Get some air. No sense in moping around here all day. I'm going to make some beef tea, and keep an ear out for Nancy while Kit gets some sleep. There's nothing useful you can do except stay out of the way.'

I trailed out of the dining room and down the hall to get my coat. The fluttering in my chest that had been constant while Mam was ill, was back, along with a certain guilty relief that I wasn't expected to *do* anything. When Mam was ill I'd *had* to cope – there was nobody else. And it had been horrific and I had failed. If Mam had had Kit knowing what to do, and someone as kind and sensible as Miss McKay, she mightn't have got so bad. She might be fine now, driving down Eupatoria Street in a charabanc, gathering all the women to go and vote, changing the world. And I'd be at her side, helping.

I pulled on my coat, as always having to disentangle the sleeve, which had got stuck in the armhole, rammed my woollen beret down on my head, and wound my new scarf round my neck. A smell of beef tea drifted out of the kitchen, making my nose wrinkle. A little snore came from upstairs. I tried to breathe in hope – Nancy had everything to make her better; it would be the most terrible bad luck if she didn't make it. Whereas Mam had had a damp room and no nurse except me, and had dragged herself to work when she shouldn't have. She hadn't been able to take to her bed at the first twinge. Neither had Minnie's mam.

Of course rich people died of the flu too – look at the Member of Parliament's son – but poorer people always suffered more.

But Sandy was right – people didn't *always* die. *He* hadn't – he'd said he'd barely even been ill. I'd felt rotten but only for a few days. And the orderlies at Sunny View were both fine now, apparently. And Charlie and Rose.

Charlie and Rose! They'd be waiting. There was no way of sending a message. Would they guess one of us was ill, or would they imagine something worse – the car overturned on the road? I couldn't leave them to worry. Worry was especially bad for Rose in her condition.

I looked into the kitchen to tell Miss McKay where I was going. It was funny to see her in there, steam from the beef tea frizzing up her sparse grey hair. She looked harassed but strangely happy – as if she liked having something to do. She smiled as she wound my scarf tighter.

I was tempted to take Kit's bicycle, mine was so awkward and heavy, but I'd promised not to without asking and I didn't want to wake her. Anyway, imagine if she needed to fetch the doctor!

Wheeling my rickety old bike round the front of the house I saw the car sitting lifeless in the drive. It was still gleaming from yesterday, apart from a few streaks made by the rain. Poor car! This wasn't the glorious election expedition I'd planned. Not much of a legacy for Mam. I ran a sad finger down one of the rain streaks, remembering the terror of that first time Nancy had taken me out in the car, up over the mountain road. I remembered driving home, watching what Nancy's hand and feet did, sure that it couldn't be too difficult. And now I knew the roads so well. And there was never much traffic apart from bikes and carts. Nancy wasn't a great driver, but she'd never actually bumped into anything.

How hard could it be?

You're never scared. You always see how things can be done.

I leaned the bike against the wall. *I'll just try the starting handle,* I thought. *To see if I can. Probably I'll do it wrong, and nothing will happen.* I grabbed the starting handle. It was much heavier than I'd imagined. I gave it a good yank and then another one. I cranked at it until the engine stuttered and roared. Someone will come and tell me to stop, I thought. They'll hear the racket. But nobody came. The front of the house was blank and silent. I opened the car door, lowered myself into the driving seat and peered through the windscreen. The driveway looked funny from behind the bonnet, faraway and too close at the same time. I looked down at the pedals at my feet. I knew there was something for starting and something for stopping. And another one – I wasn't sure what that was for.

Gently I pressed the first pedal and the car leapt forward, juddering over the pebbly gravel with a very serious-sounding crunch. I was intoxicated with delight and power. All I had to do was steer, and if I could steer my old bike I could steer anything! I pulled down on the steering wheel and the car tipped to the left. It felt like a huge monster, roaring, out of control, and the gatepost reared up – where had that come from? I rammed my foot down on what I hoped was the brake but the car roared louder and took another jolt forward. I hauled the wheel round and avoided the gatepost, and then – oh God! Someone – a person! Waving their arms. Yelling 'Stop, for Christ's sake! The brake! The middle one.'

Somehow my foot found the brake and forced down on it. The car stopped with a jolt that shuddered through every bone in my body and the engine coughed and died.

I collapsed over the wheel in relief.

'What on earth are you trying to do? Bloody hell, Stella – I didn't survive the Western Front to be mown down in the driveway!'

It was Sandy. I noted with interest that fury didn't always look red; it could look very white. Perhaps he'd been a bit afraid too?

I tried to explain but my voice wouldn't come. My breathing was rapid and shallow, and something huge battered at my chest. It must have been my heart; I hadn't realised it could do that.

'Stella?'

I swallowed. 'I promised to take Rose to vote,' I said. 'Nancy can't drive her because she has flu – I was right. So I thought I would. I didn't want to let her down.'

He shook his head. Colour was slowly returning to his face. 'You make it sound – almost – reasonable,' he said. 'But – forgive me if I'm wrong, but you can't actually drive, can you?'

'Not exactly. It was harder than it looked,' I admitted.

Sandy's breath was coming in whooshing gasps. 'I saw you from the window. I thought my eyes were playing tricks. Or else I'd finally gone mad. So I came down to see – well, to stop you. I thought you were going to run me down.'

'I was getting the hang of it.'

He raised his eyebrows. 'Let me in. I'll take it back round to the side of the house. You're lucky I'm the only one spotted you.'

I shifted over to the passenger seat. I'd rather have got out, but I didn't think I could actually stand. Sandy cranked up the starting handle, then lowered himself in beside me and put the car into a smooth reverse.

'You drive well,' I said.

'Of course.'

'Why *of course*? Because you're a man?'

'Because I learnt in the army.' He looked over his left shoulder. His face was very intent, but the car slid backwards obediently. 'You're lucky you didn't crash,' he said. 'You could have smashed up the car, never mind yourself.'

'I didn't expect it to feel so powerful,' I said. 'It sort of got away from me.'

When he had settled the car back in its parking space – it was only a few feet; it had felt much further – Sandy sprang out and went round to open the passenger door for me. I stayed where I was.

'Stella?'

'Get back in,' I said.

'Why?'

'For a minute. Please.'

'If you think I'll give you a driving lesson, after –'

'No. I don't think I'm ready to learn to drive just yet. Please?'

He sighed but got back in beside me. 'What?' he asked.

'This is the first time you've been outside since – well, for ages.'

'A month and a day.'

'How does it feel?'

'To be honest, I've been too busy trying not to get killed by a rampant girl car-thief to think about how it *feels*.' He pulled a cigarette out of his pocket, a sure sign that he was prepared to stick around for a bit though very possibly also a reaction to his near-death experience. 'I'm fine,' he said. 'Just let me get used to being alive.'

Ask him. The worst he'll do is say no.

You can't. Look what happened the last time he tried to go anywhere. What if he panics and crashes the car? What if he just freezes, like last time?

At least you'd have tried.

'Sandy? Can I ask you something?'

He flicked ash over the door.

'I know you don't like going anywhere –'

'It's not a matter of *liking*.'

'I know. But today – it's *so* important. Rose fought all her life to be able to vote. My mam did too. I can't bear not being able to help. She'll be sitting up at the farm now, waiting – expecting –'

'You want me to give you a lift?'

'Um …' I'd been going to ask him to go and pick them up, and I would meet them in town. But I saw how impossible that would be. He had no idea where he was going, and that was the least of his worries.

So I nodded. He rested his hands on the steering wheel. The cold air was reddening the skin round his knuckles. His nails were bitten short.

'I know it'd be hard for you,' I said. 'It's quite a long way to the farm – about four miles. And then into the town. Which will be crowded with people voting I expect. And then all the way back. It's a lot to ask.' I chewed the end of a piece of hair. 'And I know the election doesn't mean that much to you.'

'It did to Helen,' he said quietly. He leaned back in the seat and rested his hand on the top of the door. He drummed his fingers. It was an irritating noise but I nobly forbore to complain. I could hear both of our breathing – mine was getting back to normal but anticipation caught in my chest.

'She would have loved seeing women vote today.' His voice was so quiet I could hardly hear it. 'I don't think her mother will.'

'She might make the effort,' I suggested. 'In Helen's memory.'

He shook his head.

'But *you* can?'

'I'm registered at home in Belfast, not here. So – no, I can't.' He stared ahead for ages, his good eye fixed on the middle distance. I was willing him so hard that I thought he must feel it. And then he seemed to make up his mind. He placed his hand on the door-handle, pushed open the door, and stepped out of the car. Before I had time to say or do anything to stop him, he was walking back towards the house, leaving me alone in the car.

33

Disappointment and anger fought it out in my head. All I could do now was get out of the car, retrieve the bike, and cycle up to tell Rose the bad news.

I opened the door and stepped out on to the gravel, my boots crunching. I had just slammed the door shut when Sandy came round the side of the house, dressed in his overcoat and tweed cap, swinging a pair of driving goggles from one hand. He frowned when he saw me.

'You haven't changed your mind?' he asked.

'I thought – it doesn't matter!' I jumped back in. 'Let's go!'

At first Sandy drove so slowly that I could have screamed. The car nosed out of the driveway; crept down the loaning; crawled towards the crossroads. I didn't scream: I kept very, very quiet, terrified of putting him off. The only sound was the putter of the engine. As we approached the crossroads, the memory of him standing there, unable to move, unaware even where he was, stormed into my mind. I forgot my own fear; I was so focussed on keeping him going. I couldn't look at him; I fixed my eyes sternly on the road ahead, keeping up a silent litany: *Don't stop, Sandy, don't stop! Don't stop don't stop don't –*

Just before the crossroads, the car shuddered to a halt.

Sandy slumped forwards, buried his head in his hands. 'I can't,' he said. He pulled off his goggles and rested his head on the steering wheel. His breathing was ragged; he was shaking all over; he was very nearly as bad as he'd been the day of the funeral. I sat, frozen in despair. Was this how my wonderful plan was going to end?

I shook his shoulder. 'Come on,' I said. 'You *can* do it.' My voice was thin and uncertain. I forced myself to sound more confident. 'Let's try as far as that tree. See?'

I made him look up. Sweat pinpricked his face. No, it *wasn't* as bad as the day of the funeral: he wasn't spouting nonsense about trenches. 'You don't have to think about the whole journey,' I said. 'Just one bit at a time. Remember we looked at the sky? Remember we saw the stars coming, one by one? Star by star? That's how we have to do it.'

'I can't.' His voice was muffled. He swallowed hard. 'It's not like we *have* to. It's not a matter of life and death.'

'Things don't have to be a matter of life and death to be important.'

Sandy said nothing. I thought of how much his life *had* been about life or death. Wondered if he had actually killed someone, and what that must do to a person. Those hands gripping the steering wheel had held a gun.

'*Helen* would have said it mattered,' I ventured.

Sandy took out his handkerchief and wiped the sweat off his face. He put his goggles back on.

'Right,' he said. 'Let's keep going. But don't sit there all silent, like Patience on a monument. You make me nervous.'

'I was *trying* not to distract you,' I said with dignity. At least he hadn't noticed *my* fear!

'I need distraction. Talk nonsense. Anything. Just keep chattering.'

'That's the opposite of what I'm normally asked to do.'

But I didn't mind. I would have talked for a week if it would get Rose to the polling station.

The drive felt endless. I forced myself to chatter. Mostly nonsense. I was scared that if I stopped, Sandy would come over all funny again. Or I would. I couldn't believe he couldn't see me shaking. I had to yell and sometimes repeat myself over the drone of the engine. We got safely past the tree, and another tree, and Sandy's hands started to grip the steering wheel less tightly, and his breathing started to sound less ragged.

Soon I had something else to worry about. I'd been so scared of being scared that I'd nearly forgotten. But as we turned off into the hills and the roads started their up-and-down twists and swoops, the hateful queasiness started. I kept talking, hoping I could distract it into submission, but after one plunging hill black spots danced in front of my eyes and my insides spun.

'Stop!'

'But this can't be it – there's no farm here.'

'Gonnabesick,' I managed, my hand clamped to my mouth.

'Oh, help!' He wrenched the wheel, stood hard on the brake and we jerked to a stop just in time for me to scramble out.

It was much as before; it might even have been the same gateway. Sandy wasn't much use; he sort of hopped about at a safe distance. Eventually I staggered back and leaned against the car.

'You did once mention you got sick in cars,' Sandy said. 'But I assumed you were being dramatic.'

'No.' I breathed in the cold mountain air.

'You wanted to do this, *knowing* you'd be sick?'

I nodded. 'I'd forgotten how horrible it was,' I admitted. 'And how scary. Look.' I held out my hand. It was shaking. For some reason I didn't mind him knowing. 'Actually,' I said, 'I hate cars.'

He rubbed his hands over his face. 'We're as crazy as each other,' he said.

'Look at how far we've come.' I gestured down the valley. Far below us you could just make out the town, a tiny grey huddle curled up between the hills' armpit and the open sea. The road behind us was a thin curving ribbon between the green hills, and ahead of us the stone-walled fields marched beside the road and up the sides of the high mountains where they gave way to rough scree. A huge milky sky covered it all.

I pointed down at the town. 'People will be queuing up to vote now,' I said. 'Men *and* women. Many for the first time. Having their say in the future. And two more people will be able to do it because of *us*. Now, let's get going again. It's just the next lane.'

We reached the farm safely. Sandy let out a low whistle as he drove up the pitted track between the fields. 'That's a lot of work for one man.'

Rose came out of the kitchen door when the car pulled up. She had a good navy coat on, though it didn't button over her belly, and a little hat with a feather. 'There you are!' she said.

'I'm sorry we're so late. We got delayed by – well, a couple of things.' I frowned at Sandy, hoping he wouldn't go into details. 'Sandy Reid. Rose Sullivan.'

'Rose Maguire now.' They shook hands, and Rose said, 'So Nancy changed her mind after all?'

'No!' I said. 'She's got flu.'

'Oh, dear God.' Rose clutched her throat.

'Is your husband ready?' Sandy asked. I could see him trying not to look at Rose's belly.

'He's about the yard. He thought you weren't coming. I told him he'd get his good clothes ruined – but he said he couldn't afford to waste the day.' She smiled at me. 'I knew you wouldn't let us down.' She looked at the car. 'That's some beast of a thing,' she said. 'We'll feel like royalty going down the town in that!'

Charlie came round the corner. He spread his hands. 'I didn't get myself dirtied. I only fixed thon wee bit of wall. I'll just wash my hands and change my cap.' He nodded at Sandy and Rose explained. They looked at each other in the way strange dogs do. Sandy must be ten years younger, I thought, and yet he would have led men like Charlie into battle. They shook hands.

While Charlie was in the house Sandy mortified me by telling Rose what had happened on the way. Her eyes widened in concern. 'Och, Stella,' she said, 'you do look pale. Why don't you stay here while we're in town? No sense in putting yourself through all that.'

I can't pretend I wasn't tempted. I didn't think I'd ever get used to motoring, and car-sickness was a good excuse, as well as being so miserable and humiliating in its own right. It was a long way into town. I'd be lucky to escape without another bout. And it's not like they *needed* me. *I* couldn't vote. If I stayed here I could do something useful. If Sandy didn't know the way to town, Rose or Charlie could direct him.

But they were strangers. And neither had any idea of the effort it took Sandy to keep going. What if he had another attack of nerves?

'No,' I said. 'D'you think I'd let you have all the adventure without me? I'll be fine – and don't worry, if I need to stop I'll yell out in plenty of time.' I made my voice as bright as I could.

'I was sick for weeks with the baby,' Rose said. Sandy blushed. 'Chewing ginger helped. There's some in the pantry. Run in and get it, love. It's in a jar on the middle shelf.'

When I got back out – I stopped for a quick drink of water – they were all arguing about who should sit where in the car. Rose thought Charlie would be more comfortable in front because of his leg, but he said she should sit in front because of the baby.

Sandy shifted from one leg to the other. 'Er,' he said, 'the baby? It's not *imminent*, is it?'

Rose laughed. 'It's not due till March.'

'Good. We've had enough adventures getting this far.'

Charlie clambered into the back beside me. Maybe because of the ginger, I survived the mountain roads, and once the car was speeding down the straight, smooth road into town I let myself relax. It was too noisy to have much conversation but I caught a few words from the front seat – 'suffragette – vote – prison – really believe – so kind – poor Nancy –'

A blond tendril of hair had escaped from Rose's hat and curled on her neck above the collar of her coat.

Charlie put his hand out and touched it. 'This means the world to her,' he said. 'She's fought so hard – lost so much – when I first met her she was all fight and rage! Organising the girls in the factory. They all looked up to her. I know part of her wishes she was back with them.' I think it was the most he had ever said to me.

I nodded. 'Like my mam,' I said. 'She would have – today – well, you know.'

'Aye.' He gave me a funny sort of look. 'You're very like her,' he said.

'You said you never met her.'

He looked confused. 'I meant Rose. You're very like Rose.'

'Well,' I said, 'that's not surprising, is it?'

Before he could answer, we were pulling up outside the parish hall. A white placard was tied to the railings announcing POLLING STATION. A man in a tweed cap came out, then a stout woman. The woman smiled at us, and I wondered if she had the same history-making feeling that I had.

'Here you are,' Sandy said.

I watched them go in, Charlie limping badly but with his head held high; Rose on his arm, clumsy with the child, but proud too. They'd both fought, and both suffered, but whatever happened in Ireland's future, today they were triumphant, having their say in it for the first time.

34

Rose and Charlie came out of the polling station, arm in arm. Rose's face was like a star.

'We'd like to take you to tea,' she said, 'to say thank you.'

'It was nothing,' Sandy said.

Rose gave him a keen look. 'That's not true.'

'The hotel's closed.'

'The Cosy Kettle isn't,' I said. 'Look – that couple just went in.'

'Public places are meant to be closed,' Sandy said.

'Well, some aren't,' I said. 'But *we've* all had the flu. I'd love a cup of tea. All that ginger's burnt the mouth off me!'

I wished I could tell him what he evidently hadn't picked up on: *They want to treat us. No, they probably can't afford it. But they want it to be more equal. It will please them.* I tried to show this with my eyes. I failed.

He just said, 'Are you feeling sick again, Stella? You look funny.'

'I could do with some air,' I said. 'Why don't you and Charlie go on into the Cosy Kettle?' I suggested to Rose. 'We'll join you very shortly.'

I grabbed Sandy's arm so he couldn't escape and we set off along the seafront. I liked the feeling of my arm in his; it felt like having a big brother. And the few people we passed looked at him with admiration: he was tall and I suppose people could tell from his eye that he was a wounded soldier.

We leaned on the iron railings. The sea was grey but a glitter of afternoon sun played on its surface.

'It's the same view as from my window,' Sandy said. 'Only it feels different from here.' He breathed a lungful of air. 'We used to come here when I was a kid. Seaside holidays. We stayed in a boarding house just opposite the harbour.'

'I didn't know that.' But then, I didn't actually know much about him.

'It's one reason I stayed on here when I left Sunny View. I was always so happy here.'

'But,' I ventured, 'you never actually *came* into town, did you? I mean, you might have been anywhere.'

'No. The longer I stayed in – well, you saw how it was. It's like I stood still that day in France – the day I told you about – and then I couldn't get moving again. I was sort of frozen.'

'But not now?'

He didn't say anything for some time. 'Thanks to you,' he said.

'*I* didn't do anything! Only bully you a bit.'

He traced the pattern on the ironwork. For once he didn't have a cigarette in his hand. 'You didn't *just* bully me. You were kind and –'

'*Everyone* was kind, Sandy. You can't say they weren't. The whole house was organised around you. Captain Reid this, Captain Reid that.'

He looked embarrassed. 'I didn't know.'

'No, you were too busy being the madman in the attic.'

He didn't reply to this, and I wondered if I'd offended him. 'Not that I think you're mad,' I rushed on.

'*Neurasthenic* is the word.' He frowned. '*Nervous*.'

'You weren't nervous today,' I said. 'Not once we got going. You were really brave.'

'Thanks to you.'

I wasn't going to argue with this and get all falsely modest and coy. 'We were a good team,' I said.

'But you were brave too. You were nearly as scared as me – *and* you knew you'd be sick – but you still did it.'

I shrugged. 'It wasn't *brave* like – well, like you.'

'There's more than one kind of bravery.'

'True.' I thought about Rose, and Mam, and how brave they'd both been in their fight for women's rights. And Mam never really got to see the end of that fight, but Rose did. Her face when she came out after voting! I smiled. 'It was worth it,' I said. 'I wonder how many people in that polling station have a story to tell?'

'Everyone,' he said. 'Especially now. The war, the flu, independence – what's going to happen in Ireland. There's so much going on. You can't get your head round all of it at once.'

'Like the sky,' I said. 'You can only grasp it star by star.' I thought of all the women voting today, every vote brightening the future, like stars pricking through the darkness one by one.

'I'm going home,' Sandy said.

'But Rose and Charlie are waiting in –'

'Not now,' he said. 'I mean – home to Belfast. My family's lost Helen. They shouldn't have to lose me too.'

'But …' *I want you to stay here! I want you to make friends with Rose and Charlie and go and help on the farm! You can't spoil my great plan.*

Aloud I said, 'When?'

'Tomorrow. I'll take the train.'

'For ever?'

He shrugged. 'It's time I got back to some kind of normal life. I'm fit enough.'

'A few weeks of farm work would set you up better,' I said. 'You can't *really* say you've had the benefit of the good sea air. And why would you want to go to the city? It's full of flu germs. Don't you read the papers? I'm sure your family would rather have a nice letter reassuring them how much better you are and promising to visit when the flu's over.'

He laughed. 'Stella! You're trying to organise me.'

'I can't help it.' My voice was mournful. 'It's what I do.'

'I hope it always will be,' he said. 'But you need something big.'

I looked out at the rippling sea. If Sandy was going to Belfast, I could go too. Not to be with him – though it would be quite nice to visit and tell him my adventures – but to start that something big.

But Nancy was ill. And when she got better – I crossed my fingers, not to tempt fate – she'd need help with the business. And I didn't want to leave Rose and Charlie either, not just yet, especially now I knew they were family.

'I will do something big one day,' I said. 'But I can't start yet.' I kicked the sea wall in frustration. 'Ouch!'

'Oh, Stella.' For the first time Sandy gave a laugh that wasn't bitter. 'Can't you see you already have?'

Acknowledgements

Thanks, in the first place, to Siobhán Parkinson and Gráinne Clear at Little Island, for wanting to publish a story about women's suffrage, for trusting me to write it, and for loving it so much. *Star by Star* has been my happiest writing experience ever, in no small part owing to your enthusiasm. Faith O'Grady, agent extraordinaire: thanks once again for your belief in my writing and for everything you do for my career.

The staff at the Linen Hall Library in Belfast have been, as ever, generous and enthusiastic in helping me track down old books and newspapers. *Star by Star* was mostly edited at the Tyrone Guthrie Centre at Annaghmakerrig, that refuge for which I am always thankful.

Thanks to Susanne Brownlie and Julie McDonald for commenting on early drafts; and to all my lovely friends, especially fellow writers, for succour. As always I'm wary of mentioning names and forgetting someone, but if you think I mean YOU then I do. Booksellers, reviewers and readers – thanks for supporting my books, and I

WWW.DOLLARAMA.COM

DOLLARAMA

5095 Yonge Street Unit B8
Toronto ON M2N 6Z4
(416)225-1933
HST 863624433

ACQUOT DARK   667888095155   1.50 H

UBTOTAL $1.50
ST 13% $0.20
OTAL $1.70
MASTERCARD $1.70

YPE: PURCHASE

CCT: MASTERCARD

MOUNT: $ 1.70

ARD NUMBER: ************6895
ATE/TIME: 19/02/27 15:19:49
EFERENCE #:   66260826 0010013970 T
UTHOR. #:   08476S

    01/027 APPROVED - THANK YOU

    NO SIGNATURE TRANSACTION

      -- IMPORTANT --
Retain This Copy For Your Records

    *** CUSTOMER COPY ***

===
            NO EXCHANGE
            NO RETURN
THANK YOU FOR SHOPPING AT DOLLARAMA

019-02-27 15:19:54
00800 01 269068   3879

hope it's not presumptuous to thank you in advance for championing this latest one.

Thanks to my parents, John and Poppy Kerr, for their steadfast belief in me: like Stella, I always wanted to do great things and you always made me believe I could. My school, Victoria College, also helped foster my feminism and self-belief, and once again I remember with gratitude my history teacher Alison Jordan, who lit the spark that flamed my love for history.

Finally, I'm always grateful to the many brave women throughout history who have fought for a better future for us all, and who continue that fight around the world. Stars, every one.

About the Author

Sheena Wilkinson has been described as 'one of our foremost writers for young people' (*The Irish Times*, March 2015). Since the publication of the multi-award-winning *Taking Flight* in 2010, she has published several acclaimed novels, including *Grounded*, which won the overall Children's Books Ireland Book of the Year in 2013. Her first historical novel, *Name upon Name*, set in 1916 Belfast, was chosen as Waterford's 'One Community, One Book' title. Sheena lives in County Down, where she spends her time writing, singing and walking in the forest thinking up more stories.